VISIONS OF THE HEART

When property developer Connor Grant contracted Natalie Jensen to landscape the grounds of his large country house near Ashley in South Australia, she was ecstatic. But then she discovered he was acquiring — and ripping apart — great swathes of the town. Her own mother's house and the hall where the drama group met were two of his targets. Natalie was desperate to stop Connor's plans — but she also had to fight the powerful attraction flowing between them.

*Books by Christine Briscomb
in the Linford Romance Library:*

GENTLEMAN'S AGREEMENT

CHRISTINE BRISCOMB

VISIONS OF THE HEART

Complete and Unabridged

LINFORD
Leicester

First published in Great Britain in 1992 by
Robert Hale Limited
London

First Linford Edition
published 1999
by arrangement with
Robert Hale Limited
London

British Library CIP Data

Briscomb, Christine
    Visions of the heart.—Large print ed.—
    Linford romance library
    1. Love stories
    2. Large type books
    I. Title
    823.9'14 [F]

    ISBN 0–7089–5448–0

Published by
F. A. Thorpe (Publishing) Ltd.
Anstey, Leicestershire

Set by Words & Graphics Ltd.
Anstey, Leicestershire
Printed and bound in Great Britain by
T. J. International Ltd., Padstow, Cornwall

This book is printed on acid-free paper

1

'No, no! For heaven's sake, you're in love with each other! You haven't seen her for six weeks, Adrian. Put a bit more *feeling* into it.' Natalie Jensen ran an anguished hand through her hair.

'But she's — she's . . .'

'She's what?'

'She's a limp rag. When I hold her she sort of — sags.'

Natalie thumped heavily up the stairs at the side of the stage and stood glaring at them, her hands on the hips of her jeans. Cripes, why did she ever agree to get involved in amateur dramatics? 'Sandra, could you respond a bit more? Look as if you enjoy being in his arms?'

Sandra pouted. 'Well, I don't! Peter would have been a lot better in the part. I've a good mind to pull out of the whole thing.'

1

Natalie sighed. 'It's too late to pull out now — opening night is only three weeks away. Take it again from the top of page forty-four — where the aunt goes out.'

She turned from the brightly-lit stage and resumed her place in the auditorium. 'O.K.' she said wearily, 'roll it!'

A few words of dialogue and then the clinch. A clinch meeting only at the shoulders. 'No! You look like a church steeple — wide at the base.' Natalie heard a chuckle from behind her. She whirled around, her corn-coloured hair flying in an arc.

In the dark at the back of the hall, two eyes gleamed in amusement. She'd noticed a shadow earlier, but passers-by often dropped in when The Limelighters were rehearsing. As long as they kept quiet they were never turfed out — a bit of word-of-mouth publicity never did any harm. Ashley was a small town and they needed all the attention they could get to fill the hall for four nights.

Natalie turned back to the stage. 'How many times do I — ' and she ran up the stairs.

Footsteps followed her. Light, quick footsteps bringing a tall figure onto the stage. She swung around angrily.

But he was too quick for her. 'Look!' he said to the other two standing with open mouths. And strong arms snaked around Natalie, one across her shoulders and the other around her waist. She started to splutter but his mouth came down, soft but unyielding, on hers.

For an instant, he raised his head and said sternly, 'Put your arms around my waist,' and then his warm lips were on hers again. Since he was bending her backwards as if her spine were rubberized, she did as she was told, but stiffly. Better that, she thought hazily, than they should both crash onto the stage.

His head came up again. 'Put some *feeling* into it!' Brown, alert eyes glinted as he repeated her earlier words. And as his lips met hers again, she tightened her hold on his muscled back. He felt warm and he felt fit. Then her mind recoiled, horrified, at the knowledge that the kiss was having an effect — a powerful effect — on her heartbeat.

After a moment, he released her and stood back. 'What do you think? That's how you want it, don't you?' Earnest face, disarmingly serious, but a gleam in the eye that he didn't attempt to hide.

Sandra gave a giggle at the double-entendre. Natalie swung around, a little wobbly on her feet, and glared at the girl. Sandra choked on another giggle and Natalie transferred her glare to the stranger.

'Do you mind not interfering?' Not as firmly in control as she would have liked — in fact, her voice had a distinct tremor. She'd not been held like that since Gary had . . . She took a deep breath and focused her thoughts on the present.

'This is not a public performance. I'll have to lock the doors in future if — '

He shrugged and held out his hands in apologetic appeal. 'Sorry, sorry!' He didn't look it. He looked amused and unrepentant. But he turned and took the steps in two bounds. 'I'll call in tomorrow and see you at the office.' And he was gone.

'Who was *that*?' breathed Sandra in the silence.

'No idea. And he's of no consequence — let's get on.' But, happily, he had been of some consequence to Adrian, she thought, as he bravely took the girl in his arms and pulled her towards him firmly in the same way the stranger had done with Natalie. He looked as if he enjoyed having the upper hand.

'Good — great!' praised Natalie. But her mind wasn't in it. Damn the man! She didn't want to resurrect any of those feelings. They were dead and buried — weren't they? Three years was a long time but it had taken all of that. She was independent and loving it and no-one was going to change things.

'Coffee!' she announced ten minutes later. And as she turned on the jug, she shook her head at Sandra. 'You're still not sure of your lines. Take Act Three. Can you put some more — ah — effort into getting it right? If your uncle's coming all the way from Melbourne to look us over, you'd better be word perfect. Get Peter to hear your lines.'

'Peter's still huffy about not getting the lead.' The girl glared at Adrian.

'He can't always get the best parts, Sandra. It was time for Adrian to score.'

But as she locked the door to the dark hall behind her later that night, she wondered whether Adrian had enough life in him for the part. Certainly he'd sparked up a bit after the demonstration by the stranger. Her stomach lurched at the memory. She'd got a whiff of newly-showered male, a soapy, refreshing smell, and the very slightest suggestion of stubble against her skin.

She shivered in the cool April air. Snap out of it, Natalie! He's just an over-confident stranger who thinks that a small South Australian country town is the place to impress himself on the natives. And then his final words came back to her. 'I'll come and see you tomorrow in your office.'

He wanted some landscaping done? He hadn't seemed the type to be settling in a country town. And how had he known where she was? He must have seen the note on the office door, she decided, inserting the ignition key into the Suzuki. She shrugged and turned the key.

★ ★ ★

Natalie opened the window to let in the warm morning air. Last night seemed a long time ago. 'Hamish! Coffee? I want a break and I need an excuse.'

'Slacking again?' The burly Scotsman,

built like an ox, straightened his back and grinned at her. 'Be there in five.' And he gave the piece of rock a resounding whack with his hammer.

She never slacked and he knew it. The real difficulty lay in trying to stop herself working. There were the hospital grounds to be planned and costed by the end of the month so the administrator could present the details to the Board at the next meeting. And there was the waterfall for Mrs Travers' garden — she wanted it installed before her relatives from interstate visited in June. Probably impossible, but Natalie had to try for the old lady's sake.

And there was the need for some landscaping to be done around the theatre. The Limelighters needed something going for them — the old hall was not exactly a thing of beauty. She had promised to contribute the labour and material so the place would look a bit smarter. Sandra had bribed her uncle to make the journey for the opening night — 'Uncle Jeremy's in films' she'd said airily.

Natalie grinned as she turned on the coffee machine. Amateur theatre was fun — most of the time — and she enjoyed channelling some of her creative energy into directing but — yoicks! — let's not get carried away.

She found two mugs, looking sordid with dregs from yesterday — she really must organize herself better — and washed them in the tiny sink. If I can just finish that rough sketch of the land around the theatre, I can get Hamish to collect the moss rocks and I can start tomorrow. Cost will be a bit steep, but . . .

Natalie looked around the pre-fabricated shed that was her office, her workroom and, at the moment, her home. If only she could get one, just one, spectacular success, she'd be on her way to making a name.

Out of the corner of her eye, she saw a movement outside. A dark blue sports car slid to a whispering halt. Sleek and smoothly sophisticated, it had a driver to match. She watched the tall figure uncoil himself from the car and lock the door, staring at the building as he did so.

He strode up the brick-paved winding path, between the clumps of budding bronze chrysanthemums and the sprawling ground cover plants and disappeared around the side.

The door burst open and he was inside, his eyes taking in at one sweeping glance the filing cabinets, her desk littered with half-finished drawings, the coffee clutter and the huge drawing-board. His gaze flicked momentarily to the mural-type poster of the Conservatory at Kew Gardens that covered one wall.

Then his lean face slowly creased. The slight stubble of yesterday had become today's six o'clock shadow — definitely later than five o'clock, she noted. And he was, without doubt, too dreamy-looking for his own good.

'Hullo . . . !' The second syllable was

loaded with innuendo and appreciation — got it down to a fine art, she decided. 'We meet again. And you look as terrific first thing in the morning as last thing at night.'

Such brilliant repartee, she thought, one hand in the pocket of her jeans and the other holding a dripping mug.

'I should have introduced myself last night. The name's Connor Grant.' He announced himself as if he expected her to cheer. Natalie looked at him balefully.

He seemed not the slightest bit concerned about the unwelcoming silence in the room. 'I'd like to see Mr Jensen. Is he around?'

'Natalie Jensen,' she said.

'No, no!' He gave her another broad smile. 'Jensen and MacIntyre, landscape gardeners, right? Joe Chalmers recommended Nat Jensen. Is he around?'

'It's Natalie and it's me. Joe always calls me Nat.'

He stared at her for five long seconds while she noted with satisfaction that his bristly bottom jaw had sagged a millimetre or two.

'*You?*' Dark eyes followed the sweep of corn-coloured hair to her shoulders, down her slim figure to her jean-clad hips, long legs and desert boots and then focused again on her face. He gave a huge sigh.

'I thought you were the secretary,' he said, only slightly abashed. 'The card pinned to the door — last night — it said: 'The workhorse is at rehearsals' so I thought — Oh dear!' He grinned.

'It was a joke — to tell Hamish — I didn't expect anyone else to call.'

'You're Jensen? But I wanted someone who could — ' His voice tailed off.

She put down the mug carefully. 'Mr Grant, I am fully-trained and experienced and if Joe Chalmers recommended the firm, then you should have faith — he's not exactly the world's easiest man to please.'

'But rocks and things . . . '

'It's not all heave-and-grunt these

12

days,' she said patiently. 'Mechanization has arrived in Australia. However,' she turned away and picked up the mug again, 'I'm not about to try to persuade you to do anything rash, like giving a commission to a woman.'

She drew the stool towards the drawing-board and concentrated stonily on some notes pinned to it. She sensed, rather than saw, his agony of indecision. His dark eyes looked around the room again, resting briefly on the pencilled sketch in front of her.

'Well . . . Um . . . Do you have any photographs of your work?'

She slid off the stool, pulled out a drawer in the desk and handed him a thick ring-back folder. 'Take a seat and browse at your leisure,' she invited, turning back to the board. 'We can't take credit for the whole of it, of course — nature helped.'

He turned the pages slowly, occasionally raising his eyes to look at her. She had no need to sell her work.

There were 'before' and 'after' colour photographs and under each was a potted description of what had been done and the date. The gardens were mainly around the eastern suburbs of Adelaide and some were mildly spectacular, she knew.

'Coffee?' she asked after a few moments.

'Love one!'

He reached out with long strong fingers, curling them around hers while he took the mug with his other hand. She pulled away hurriedly — so hurriedly that a few drops of the hot liquid dropped onto his moleskins. He winced, but said nothing, just giving her a speculative look from under ridiculously long eyelashes.

Her cheeks reddened. Over-reacting, that's what you're doing, Natalie Jensen. It was just an accidental touch, no need to panic. What's the touch of a hand, when last night he'd taken you in his arms? Suddenly the office seemed too small for both of them — there was no

14

place to escape. Escape? Why should I want to escape?

She heard Hamish's heavy footsteps outside. His big frame filled the doorway as he clumped in and then stopped short. She was never more pleased to see him.

'Mr Grant, this is Hamish MacIntyre. Hamish, Connor Grant.'

The big fellow held out a beefy hand. 'Gidday!' It always amused Natalie to introduce Hamish. With a name like that people expected a broad Celtic inflection with clipped vowels. He had inherited his 'braw' Highland physique and colouring from his parents but he was as Australian as Fosters' beer.

Connor Grant turned and shook his hand energetically. 'Perhaps we can discuss what it is I'm wanting and then you could come out to my place and — '

Hamish interrupted. 'You'd better discuss things with Natalie. She's the Chief.' He gave a broad grin. 'I'm just an Indian.'

The doubtful look returned to Connor Grant's face. He's really having problems, thought Natalie gleefully. Hasn't he caught up with equal opportunity?

Hamish's face showed his amusement. He gulped the coffee and thumped down the mug, wiping his mouth with the back of his hand. 'Well, I'll leave you two to talk business and get those moss rocks. Where do you want them unloaded, Nat?'

'At the front of the place please, Hamish — some each side of the main door. And I told Mick Farrant the medium size will do. I can manage them better.'

The big fellow ambled out of the door winking at Natalie as he closed it behind him.

Connor Grant started to move around the room, his coffee mug in one hand. 'I need to think about this.'

Natalie shrugged. 'Take your time. But now, if you don't mind,' she said airily, 'I must get on. Just let me know whether you want to go ahead with your garden-planning and we can talk again.' She turned back to the drawing board.

He chuckled. 'Well, it's not exactly a 'garden' — but yes, I'll let you know.' He leant against the desk, watching her over the rim of the mug.

She drew the curved outline of a path and a stylized outline of a tree half shading it. Still he sat and watched her.

'Where did you train?'

'Melbourne School of Horticulture, the Royal Botanical Gardens at Kew, Kalmthout Arboretum in Belgium, followed by work on estates in Scotland and Italy.' She spoke crisply, thoroughly enjoying flaunting her achievements in front of him. Another commission would be useful but — from this guy? Might be tricky.

'Mm. Impressive.' He put down his mug and moved closer, looking over her shoulder at the sketch. 'And who's that one for?'

'A client,' she said calmly. 'I never

discuss my work with anyone who isn't closely concerned with the project.'

'Admirable policy,' he drawled, without moving away.

He was so close that she could feel an animal warmth emanating from him and his breath warmed her cheek. It was unnerving. She didn't want to be physically close to anyone just now. She wanted to stay aloof, no emotion and no passion, no doubts and no uneasiness. She moved slightly to one side.

But he pointed to a scribbled outline of a pond and asked a question and shuffled his feet and was close again.

She turned away abruptly. 'Look, I'm very busy. I suggest that you go away and think about what you want and then let me know.'

'That's not the way to get clients, you know,' he said mildly, putting down the empty mug. 'Aren't you supposed to sell me the idea of a woman landscaper?'

His hands were rammed into his

pockets as he perched on the edge of the desk, long legs outstretched and crossed at the ankle, relaxed now and, she noted, radiating confidence.

Natalie pushed a tress of corn-gold hair behind her ear and reached for her car keys. 'I don't need to 'sell' the idea at all. Joe Chalmers gave you our name and you can see from the album what work we've done. If and when you feel ready to discuss the project, I'll be happy to do so. In the meantime, I have to do some shopping.' Liar, she thought, but for her peace of mind she had to get rid of him.

'Sure, sure! Look, perhaps you could come and see the place tomorrow. We'll both have had a chance to think things over and — '

She was at the door now and pointedly holding it open for him. 'I've no need to think it over. I'll be free to start a new project in about a month's time.'

As he strolled down the path he called over his shoulder, 'It's quite easy to find. Take the main road to Lyndoch but turn off at the road to Romsey Plains. It's about a kilometre along on the left and the name's on the gate. It's called Seymour Rise.' His car sped away.

If he had said 'It's called Buckingham Palace' it couldn't have had a more devastating effect. Seymour Rise! She stood clutching the door frame and gawped as the car disappeared around the corner. Seymour Rise was his 'garden'?

She'd heard it had been sold but she had no other details. It had been on the market for months and Hamish had seen parties of people coming and going. The cottage he was renovating was in the lane about half-a-kilometre from the main gates.

Seymour Rise was a large place — about a hundred-and-fifty hectares of paddocks and a Heritage-listed homestead and outbuildings that rambled over about two acres. It had been opened to the public on one weekend about five years ago, while it was owned by the last in a long line of graziers and just before it had been sold to a business consortium who were training race-horses. Natalie had gone on a guided tour with her mother.

After the stock-market crash, the property came on the market again, the horses had to go, apparently to pay for some disastrous losses, and the house had stood empty and neglected for a year.

And he had called it 'my place'! As if it were a triple-fronted cream brick — except that there was nothing of the triple-fronted cream brick about him. She might have guessed — those closely-fitted moleskins, that Canterbury shirt and those loafers — very Gucci. My, my, Natalie — you sure took plenty notice of him! Couldn't help it — seeing he practically knocked me off my feet.

She slammed the door behind her and stalked down the path. Forget the guy — get on with something useful.

But the thought of that gracious old house and the rambling, neglected grounds surrounding it stuck with her as she drove to the other side of town. What a challenge it would be! She recalled the overgrown terraces, the long vista to Mount Memory, the rose garden and the wisteria blooms dripping from a wide covered path. The covered path led to a large and solid outside building that had not been open to the public.

What had they said it was? A machinery shed? A hay-barn? Suddenly she could see the rough stone outlines and hear the guide saying that it had been built in 1921 as a ballroom. A ballroom! Quaint relic of a bygone age — she'd love to have lived then. She could picture herself sweeping into the ballroom on the arm of a high, wide and handsome guy — or could she? Maybe not. Maybe she'd always have preferred to sweep in by herself.

The car wobbled as she grasped

the steering-wheel in excitement. The house was a magnet and she couldn't wait to get to work — what had she read in a book on landscaping? Something like: 'All great gardens have about them an air of inevitability.' She knew *exactly* what they meant.

That settles it — I will go tomorrow and present my best public relations face and help him overcome any qualms he may have. Seymour Rise — the words ran over her tongue like honey.

'Wheee!' she whooped as she sped to the theatre.

The building was the only hall in Ashley big enough to stage a play and it had all the accoutrements of the big theatres in the city. Thanks to an elderly actor, long since dead, who had retired to the town, it had been fitted out elaborately and several plays had been produced there.

There was no sign of Hamish but it was too soon, she decided. He had to take the truck to the supplier and the rocks would have to be carefully lifted by crane so as not to scrape off the moss and lichen. Some of the lichen would be lost on unloading, but she could cope with that.

The inside was dark and a little musty. Natalie walked around opening windows so that tonight's full-length rehearsal could go ahead without too many grumbles. There were mugs and there was coffee and some tea-bags. But no milk in the tiny fridge — she would dash over to the deli and get some and then back 'home' for a meal.

And still the thought of Connor Grant and the challenge that was sitting out there on the road to Romsey Plains would not leave her in peace. She could go without that smug chauvinist but she couldn't go without Seymour Rise. She'd kill for that commission.

What if he had second thoughts and got someone from the city? She shivered with apprehension as she ate the last of the spinach quiche at her desk. Had she been very rude? What exactly had she said to him? She groaned as she took her plate, turned on the hot tap in the curtained-off corner of the office and prepared to fill the sink.

There was a sudden 'splatt!', a quick flame and a puff of smoke from the ancient water-heater that supplied her shower as well as the washing-up water. Damn, damn, damn — the electrician had warned her.

Hamish would fix it. On cue, his heavy footsteps sounded on the path.

'Can't be done, Nat. It's too old — cut your losses. All we need here is an electric jug. Look, just because you want to be on the spot, you don't have to *live* here.' The large red-haired stone-mason leant against the door-frame.

'But I'm not going back home to live, I haven't got the time or the money to organize buying a house and there's nowhere in Ashley that's available for rent.' She tucked her hair behind her ear and started to stack the plates and mugs.

'Listen!' Hamish grinned at her. 'The cottage is ready — come and live with me.'

2

She let out a shriek of laughter. 'Why, Mr MacIntyre, what are you suggesting?'

He laughed with her. 'No — listen! There's plenty of room — remember the plans? It's designed as two units, so a relative can live there if needed — quite separate.'

'One of Marie's family? And when are you going to propose to Marie?'

He stopped laughing. 'I have, but she sent me away with a flea in my ear.' He turned and looked down the main street. 'It's no good, Nat, it looks as though I'll be batching all my life.'

'There are other women in the world, Hamish,' she said gently to his hunched back.

'Not for me there aren't . . . ' His voice tailed off.

If only Gary had thought like that.

She smiled grimly to herself. Gary had acted as if he was personally responsible for unlocking the sensuality in every woman within a forty-kilometre radius.

'How do you know you'd be safe with me?' she asked with a smile in her voice and the assurance of a long friendship.

He turned around with a wry look on his face. 'Because we're like brother and sister, Nat. With all the will in the world, that will never change. We know each other too well. Look, the place would be ideal for you — it's got a separate front door and you can be as independent as you like.'

'And if I occasionally cook a meal for you,' she said with a sly grin, 'you wouldn't object?'

'Right on!'

She laughed again then and glanced around the office. In the corner next to the sink the heavy velour curtain hid a camp bed. And next to that, a shower curtain concealing her primitive bathroom. She rubbed her cheek thoughtfully. 'To be honest, I have to admit this place isn't exactly the Ritz.'

'Then move out there whenever you like. You've got some furniture in store, right?'

She hesitated one brief moment. But then, 'Right! You've talked me into it — and do you really mean whenever I like?'

'What's wrong with now? One of these days the Health Inspector is going to catch on to what's happening and slap down an injunction to stop you living here.'

She nibbled at her lip and looked at the drawing-board and decided the plans could wait another day. An hour-and-a-half later, she carried the last of her saucepans into the neat little newly-painted kitchen in the cottage on the road to Romsey Plains. 'I'll get the rest of my furniture tomorrow,' she told Hamish.

'You're practically his next-door

neighbour now,' Hamish said, with a grin. He had been bowled over by the news of Connor Grant's acquisition of Seymour Rise and made almost speechless by the thought of the possible commission. He had watched her closely as she had told him about the conversation in the office that morning.

Now he had an amused look on his ruddy face. 'You really want that job, don't you?'

'Of course I want it, stupid! It's the chance to make our name — as long as I can put up with that — that — ' She ran out of polite words.

Hamish said nothing as he drove them back to the office. There was just a grin on his face that she'd noticed before.

At rehearsals that night, she stood resolutely facing the stage the whole time, willing herself not to look around at any odd scuffling noise behind her. And as she and the cast checked the windows and turned off the lights, the sudden burst of a powerful engine and the purr that grew gradually fainter was determinedly ignored.

★ ★ ★

He'd have rung her, wouldn't he? He wouldn't be wanting her to arrive at the house all bright-eyed and bushy-tailed if he'd already decided to commission someone else, would he?

Natalie spent an hour in the office, for decency's sake, before hurling herself into the Suzuki and trying not to break the speed limit to Seymour Rise. She swung the car through the impressive entrance — towering sandstone pillars supporting heavy wrought-iron gates. The green paintwork was peeling and the pot-holed driveway gave a spine-jarring ride.

It curved between claret ash and liquidambar and cypresses and she drove over a crumbling concrete bridge with the now-dry creek bed beneath. And then she turned a corner, around a eucalyptus with a trunk the size of a small house, and the pot-holes were forgotten.

Tucked into the side of the hill that gave it its name, Seymour Rise sat almost smugly, high mullioned windows looking down the valley over the terraces she remembered so well. There was a turret, with slits of windows and a weather-vane on top. On each side of the main building, extensions spread towards yet further buildings. It was a huge, rambling copy of an English manor-house, a bit frayed at the edges and with the fanciful addition of the turret.

Natalie turned off the engine and sat for a moment savouring the look of it. It badly needed a paint job but it was a terrific place. It deserved a better setting and her fingers tingled with wanting to get to work. More labour needed — I'll have to hire some from Gawler. Hamish and I couldn't tackle this alone.

What had once been manicured

terraces were blurred with overgrown and dried-out grass. At some time, new trees had been planted but without much thought of scale or proportion and the vista had been partially spoiled by — hold it, hold it! You haven't got the job yet. Don't start mentally reorganizing. But she had a vision of what it would look like — a vision that excited her.

The dark blue sports car was under the portico and she parked a respectable distance away on gravel that had seen better days. And as she eased herself out of the Suzuki, she crossed fingers of both hands. Let him give me this commission! I'll put up with his patronizing manner, his sickening self-confidence, his warped sense of humour — just as long as I can get my hands on this place.

The heavy brass knocker on the peeling black paint of the front door was an anachronism — she hadn't seen one since she was a child — but effective. The three-metre high door swung open and Connor's dark eyes looked into hers.

'Come in, come in!' He stood back and watched with an amused expression as she stepped inside. 'So you haven't had second thoughts?'

'No. Have you?'

'Of course not! Once I'd got used to the idea that . . . ' His voice tailed off. 'That is — there's no reason why you shouldn't be a crash-hot landscape designer.'

Oh, hurrah! He's coming on nicely. She hid a smile.

The hallway was vast, with a centrally-placed stairway leading to the upper level and dividing half-way. But it was bare and grimy and he apologized as he led her to the back of the hall and under the stairway. 'I'm cocooned back here, in what were the housekeeper's rooms and the kitchen.' His hand was lightly under her elbow, warm and reassuring as she peered into the gloom of the long corridor.

It was a pleasant feeling — for a

34

moment — and then she moved her elbow slightly. As he opened the door, to reveal a bright sunlit kitchen with a garden view, his grin had returned at her obvious avoidance of his touch.

'Coffee, before we start?' He moved towards the massive range set along one side of the kitchen. The original wood-fired cooker had been modernized. A battery of switches on one side, a microwave set in at waist level and a ceramic-topped cooking surface added up to a very state-of-the-art collection. He filled a fast-boil jug, and in no time a Bodum was brewing and filling the kitchen with the fragrance of its contents.

And all the time, she watched him. Broad shoulders under a cotton-knit navy polo-style shirt and the ubiquitous 'bleached-bones' moleskins. Tanned arms with muscles that looked dangerous. The bristly chin was clearly growing a beard — it was dark and shaggy today. And, to her surprise, bare feet.

The feet got to her. There was something boyish, yet intimate, in the sight of this suave, confident figure padding around on the smoothened earth-toned tiles of the kitchen — with bare feet. She looked away quickly just as he turned around with the Bodum in one hand and a carton of milk he had extracted from the huge fridge in the other hand.

'We can have it here,' he nodded at the large scrubbed oak table that dominated the room, 'or in there,' and he jerked his head towards the open door to what appeared to be a sitting-room. Two comfortable armchairs were in sight — two leather-covered battleships of armchairs with a low mahogany coffee table between.

She took a couple of steps towards the open door and the rest of the furniture came in sight. A large water-bed, she guessed, with a doona in black and white stripes flung carelessly over.

She retreated hastily and turned towards the kitchen table rather too quickly. He swung away the hot Bodum just in time but the milk carton squelched to disaster on the floor and gurgled. She leapt at it and turned it upright in time to rescue half the contents.

'You're very twitchy, aren't you?'

I'm twitchy all right — and so would you be. The sight of the black and white doona was too much. It was the clone of Gary's and deja vu made her breathless.

A few steps in the wrong direction, she thought, all those years ago — an unwillingness to appear naïve or unsophisticated — and she had succumbed to Gary's charm and his undoubted experience. What she had really succumbed to was a wish to be — well — adult. The reddening of her cheeks now as she turned towards the table had more to do with Gary than the fellow who stood with Bodum in hand and his head on one side.

Connor was not grinning now. There was a puzzled thoughtful look on his face and his nut-brown eyes were warm.

'The table, right?' and he placed the Bodum carefully on the work-worn surface and fetched two earthenware mugs and, without further comment, pressed down the plunger and poured the coffee.

He pushed one of the mugs towards her and started talking. He told her of the origins of the property, of how each of the sections had been owned by different farmers who had planted elms and poplars along the creek — trees fully grown even before the turn of the century.

'And then, in about nineteen-hundred-and-two, a small, but successful, sheep farmer bought one section and gradually acquired the adjacent properties as they came on the market until he had the lot. Shrewd fellow, eh?' His enthusiasm lit up his face. 'Got all that from a book in the library here — the recent owners left behind an amazing collection — couldn't be bothered to take it with them.' He shook his head incredulously at the thought. 'It was a bonus for me. Did you know them?'

She took a sip of the hot liquid. 'No — but I knew about them — they were the talk of the town. Lots of extra buildings going up, earthworks, horse-boxes turning up at all hours, fast noisy cars, wild parties. And then — suddenly — it all went quiet. All their plans for the stud farm crashed when the stock-market did, back in — whenever.'

She might not remember the date but she remembered the result. Her mother's allowance from her father stopped abruptly then. He had moved from Ashley after the divorce and the letters from him to Natalie had told of 'fantastic' deals, of a lifestyle that made her raise her eyebrows. And then, the news came of share values plunging and people made penniless and in heavy debt — news that meant nothing to her at first. Until the money that had turned up regularly — she had to hand him that — suddenly stopped, and her mother was looking dazed and talking about finding a job.

Connor drained his cup. 'From what I can gather, they had more cash than style — at first, anyway. There are certainly some weird additions to the place and there's something about the grounds that doesn't seem right — the swimming pool, for instance.'

'Swimming pool?' She looked at him in disbelief. 'I don't remember a swimming pool.'

He stood in one fluid movement and looked out of the window and upward. 'Up there, see?'

She joined him. About ten metres above, on the dry, grassy slope, she could make out the roofs of cabins set well back, but — swimming pool?

'We'll go there first.' He grabbed socks and desert boots from the floor and a firm, warm hand on her elbow steered her through the back door and towards stone steps leading upward, through an overgrown vegetable garden limp with neglect.

The steps were mostly well-formed and firm, but here and there the cement had broken away.

She stumbled as one step wobbled beneath her foot.

He was there to catch her, his arms around her waist in an instant, as if he had been poised. Somehow he kept his balance, holding her in front of him in a firm grip.

'OK?' It was a pleasant — no, more than pleasant — feeling. Warm strong arms held her steady and his words of concern were soft in her ear. She stood for a moment, her hair blowing silkily across his face.

'Fine, thanks,' Natalie answered shakily and his arms slackened. A flock of sulphur-crested cockatoos flew over, raucously announcing their passage. He gave her a sudden, tight smile and let go.

She swallowed hard and concentrated on the steps that now spread out to the flat, tiled surround of a swimming pool.

'Oh dear!' She stared at the water, desperately trying to steady her nerves by concentrating on mundane matters. A few stray gum leaves floated on the surface, and the aquamarine tiles lining the sides disappeared into a sludge of more leaves on the bottom. She looked up. Three large eucalypts overhung the pool and even as they stood there, a sudden swirling breeze brought down a dozen leaves into the pool.

'Very pretty — but hopeless. Not a good place for a pool. It needs to be out in the open, where there aren't overhanging trees — say, down there.' She waved her hand towards the lower level, below the house but to one side. 'It shouldn't interfere with the unity of the terraces and the vista towards Mount Memory, but it needs to be reasonably close to the house and *not* under trees.' She turned towards him and surprised an admiring look on his face. His eyes were on her hair, golden in the sun.

'Are you listening?' she asked, rather

more sharply than she meant to.

'To every word — every word!' His tone was serious but his eyes were laughing at her. 'Reasonably close to the house and not under trees, right?' he repeated. 'We'll just have to move it, won't we?' He might have been talking about a birdbath.

'Won't be simple. All that water . . . ' She shook her head thoughtfully.

'I've been told there's a natural spring just above, in the side of the hill.' He pointed to a half-hidden collection of pipes behind the cabins. 'They decided to use gravity both for filling and emptying the pool.' He pointed downhill this time, to where another jumble of pipes led away behind trees. 'Emptied into what was a rose garden, but the roses look a bit sick.'

'I'm not surprised,' Natalie said crisply. 'If the chlorination was effective, the roses would be suffering from terminal antisepsis.'

'It was all a bit haphazard, it seems, from what the agent said. They had a couple of gardeners, but . . . '

She wasn't listening. She was looking closely at a patch of green grass standing out from the dry surroundings and as she bent to feel the earth, she frowned.

'Mm . . . Haphazard's the right word. That's a leak from well below the waterline — look! No wonder the level's down.'

He squatted next to her and together they scraped a little damp earth away. The drops became a trickle. He turned his head, unnervingly close again, his face only a few centimetres from hers. So close she could see the amber flecks in his eyes.

She stood up quickly, an overwhelming feeling of panic in every bone. This couldn't be happening again, not now, not when I've recovered so well. I don't want a distraction like this.

She wedged a stone in the hole, kicked a few clods of earth over it and stamped them well in. 'That should hold it for a day or so, but it's not good. I'll get Hamish to have a look at it.'

'Well, I can leave that to you, yes?' His look was challenging as he, too, straightened up.

'Of course.' She didn't feel as confident as she sounded, but Hamish would know how and where and what.

An hour later they trudged back to the house. Connor had given her a guided tour of the outhouses and the nearby grounds. It was mostly as she had remembered but all of it overgrown and faded, with the whispery dryness of autumn. He was charmingly vague about what needed to be done, but he knew it was more than just cleaning up the weeds.

'The previous owners made lots of changes, it seems, mostly for the sake of fun, rather than gracious living,' he said with a grin, as they passed a go-cart track, with the rusting remains of a few vehicles lying about. 'And the horses, of course, meant lots of extra fences and railings — I'll want to get rid of all that.' He waved his hand towards where strips of fenced-off pasture were simmering in the sun. Some of the railings had collapsed.

'No horses?'

He shrugged his shoulders. 'I'm allergic to them — in the true sense, I mean. Come out in hives and get all choked up.' He became suddenly serious, looking out over the paddocks with a thoughtful expression. 'No, it's cattle I have a weakness for. Great lumbering, sweet-breathed, slow-moving cattle. I've got a vision of them all over that pasture — it'll look like a Constable.'

'More like a Russell Drysdale, I should think, with those eucalypts,' she responded dryly.

They went inside again. 'What do you think, Natalie?' She was glad he hadn't called her 'Nat'. That was all right for Joe Chalmers but it would have sounded odd on Connor's lips.

They stood together in what was clearly the drawing-room, looking through high windows grimy with dust. Outside, the covered walk was green-draped with the leaves of the deep-rooted wisteria that had survived without water and that would be heavy with purply-blue pendulous blossoms in the spring. Between other trees already dropping their leaves, she could just see the old ballroom.

'There's a lot of work — ' She hesitated. 'I can let you have a rough estimate in about a week, after Hamish and I have looked it over again, but — if we do everything you want to have done, it'll knock you back a bit.'

'Let me worry about that,' he said with a smile. A smile that made her take a deep breath. White teeth with all that tan — I'll bet he knows how sensational he looks.

'Are you having much done to the house? I'll need to talk with the architect or whoever before I make any changes outside.'

'Someone's coming out from Adelaide tomorrow — I'll ask him to get in touch.' He mentioned a firm of refurbishing architects that was familiar to Natalie — she had worked with them before.

Connor came to the door with her, their footsteps echoing in the bare rooms. He opened the door of the Suzuki and she climbed in.

'I've enjoyed showing you around — and I look forward to seeing more of you.' She looked at him sharply but his expression was bland. Finally he closed the door for her.

And as she drove away, she could see, in the rear-vision mirror, his sturdy figure, legs apart, hands on his hips and watching the car until she rounded the corner by the dry creek bed.

She felt exhilarated and excited — a feeling in the pit of her stomach as if she were in a fast lift descending. She couldn't wait to get back to tell Hamish — he knew how important the commission would be.

And Connor — what of him? She accelerated out of the gateway and drove slowly towards the town. He was attractive, no doubt about that. The lift in her stomach descended more rapidly as she recalled the feel of his arms around her waist, holding her safe. Yes, she guessed she could work with him — he hadn't been too smugly self-confident. Although, with the money he had spent buying Seymour Rise and now the money he would be spending on the grounds, let alone what needed to be done inside, he would have every reason to feel confident. What did he do that had accrued so much wealth?

She would have to get an advance payment — a sizeable amount — before they ordered any materials and put too much work in. She was prepared to draw plans and give an estimate but after that . . . She remembered that smart-aleck over at Levington who ticked off to some new project leaving her with four dozen advanced saplings and twenty tonnes of moss-rocks she could barely pay for. No, charming though he was, Connor Grant was going to have to front up with the money before she got too involved.

But he wasn't that sort, was he? Not the sort to let her down. If she were any judge of character at all, she'd say he was reliable as the sunrise. And probably a thoroughly nice person. Oops, what does *nice* mean?

It means, thought Natalie, slowing to a halt outside the hospital, he has integrity and he's honest and he'd never make a dodgy deal. Those dark-brown eyes were guileless and incapable of sly looks — they looked straight at you in a disconcerting way.

Come on now, Natalie Jensen, you've just given him an aura of saintliness because he had the good sense to give you the commission. She grinned at herself as she climbed down from the Suzuki and strode into the administrator's office.

'Clive, have you got a minute?'

'For you, Natalie, more than a minute! Take a seat.'

'Tell me, how detailed do the plans for the hospital grounds have to be?'

'Make them as detailed as you can. The fact that the Board is prepared to consider four different tenders shows they're going to be choosy.'

They went over the requirements of the tender carefully. Clive was an old friend and he would help as much as he could, but the bottom line was that the Board would be looking at her professionalism and a reasonable quotation as well as the aesthetic quality of her work.

'I hope you'll be bringing a party to the play — don't forget it's only three weeks away,' Natalie said as she stood up to go.

'Wouldn't miss it for the world! Especially since it'll be the last one.'

She turned back with a frown. 'The last one? I certainly hope not! The group's too talented to fall apart.'

'Where will it be performing, then?'

She stood very still and stared at the stocky middle-aged man shuffling his papers at the desk. 'Clive, what are you talking about?'

He straightened up and looked at her with startled eyes. 'You mean, you don't know? Don't you read the local rag?'

'Almost never — no time,' she answered in a flat voice. She kept staring at him. With an embarrassed expression, he started to talk again.

'Council passed the proposal about two months ago. You mean no one told you?'

'For heaven's sake, Clive, told me what?'

He sat down heavily. 'The hall's to be demolished in about a month — a developer bought it and the land behind. There's to be a factory built there.'

3

'A factory?' Her voice rose to a high-pitched squeak. 'How can they build a factory in She-Oak Road? It's zoned residential.' She paused and looked at him. 'Isn't it?'

'Well, no, I gather not. It's actually zoned light industrial.'

'But that's criminal! There are some lovely old houses along there — I was born in one and my mother's there still — are they all coming down?'

'I don't know, Natalie. But I do know some have become so run-down that they're beyond repair. The National Trust aren't interested — they aren't deemed to be of heritage value and some have been condemned. The hall was considered to be a fire risk and there was some dry rot in some of the uprights — '

'And no one was prepared to allocate

any money to replace them?' She remembered she had seen the council surveyor walking around the hall some time ago, but hadn't thought twice about it.

'Apparently not. It's hard times, Natalie. Money is short and grants are like hens' teeth.'

'But isn't there supposed to be an — an — what do they call it? An environmental impact statement or something?'

'Not for this sort of thing, Natalie. It's not necessary. It's just got to pass Council development plans and then it takes off.'

'But a *factory*!' she wailed. 'A noisy, smelly factory belching smoke and all sorts of — '

The administrator allowed himself a slight grin and interrupted her. 'No, not really. I gather it's to prepare and freeze local produce like potato chips and peas and things, for city restaurants. So it'll be a bit like a sort of — well — large kitchen,' he finished lamely.

'A large kitchen?' she spluttered. 'Clive, spare me the euphemisms.'

'But listen, Natalie. It means there'll be employment for quite a few people in the factory and a guaranteed market for the growers. We need something like that in Ashley, to stop the drain to the city.'

'Oh great! Very high-minded! Clive, it's just commercial wheeling and dealing and once the hall's gone there'll be no film screenings and no plays. That'll send people to the city, if nothing else will. And what's my mother going to do? The house is all she's got.'

'Well, I don't know, but I gather the developer has talked about the possibility of investing more money around here — he's got some big schemes planned to involve the town in the tourist industry. Bring a lot more money in.'

'For what? For more crass development? I'd have thought tourists would want to see the place in its natural state, not tarted up with tourist attractions and — *factories*! And who is this Rockefeller, this philanthropist, this — this — *Philistine*?'

'The same chap who bought Seymour Rise. A well-lined and successful developer from Melbourne. Someone called — what was his name?' Clive frowned with concentration. 'I remember now. Connor Grant.'

★ ★ ★

'Hamish, I don't believe it!' Natalie thumped the saucepan on the draining board and scowled. 'That is, I do believe it — I have to.'

'Well, how about eating this tucker before it gets cold? You spent a long time cooking it and I can't start before you do and I'm starving.'

'How can I eat when I'm feeling so angry? And you can forget the finer points of etiquette. Just get on with it.'

She prowled around the tiny kitchen,

her face red with suppressed indignation. 'He didn't say a word. He sat there for two nights watching it all going on — watching them rehearsing — and he spent two hours with me this morning and he didn't say a blind word.'

Hamish swallowed a mouthful of spaghetti and meat sauce and smacked his lips. 'This is great, Natalie. But listen, how was he to know that you didn't know? I mean, this production is coming off, isn't it? All that work won't be wasted.'

'We had plans organized for the rest of the year. One production every three months — they were to start casting the week after the play finished . . . ' Her voice tailed off and she groaned and looked at Hamish with wide eyes. 'Come to think of it — someone did make a comment but I was too busy to listen.'

'There you go then! Er — if you're not going to eat that, shall I finish it up?'

'Go ahead, go ahead,' she answered

absent-mindedly and prowled some more. 'But that's not the worst of it. Those lovely houses — my mother — ' Her voice sighed in despair. Then she thumped a fist into the palm of the other hand. 'I'm going to confront him. A factory! Instead of our little theatre — how could he?'

Hamish looked up as she shrugged on her parka. 'Hey, Nat! It's nearly dark — you're not going there *now*, are you?'

'You bet your life I am!' And she flung out of the door.

There were no lights showing in the big house — but then there wouldn't be. He was at the back, wasn't he? Probably counting his gold pieces, she thought grimly as she came to a skidding halt on the gravel.

The door knocker echoed deeply within the big house as she waited under the portico. And waited. And knocked again. Still no response.

Suddenly, she felt silly. Clearly, he wasn't at home — there was no sign of his car and the place was eerily silent.

Until, with a roar that made her jump and turn around, the low-slung car pulled up next to hers, its headlights illuminating the portico, and Connor leapt out with a large packet in his hands.

'Why, hello there! If I'd known you were coming, I'd have got two lots of takeaways.'

She got a tantalizing whiff of spicy Chinese food and her empty stomach rumbled. She ignored it. Share his food? She'd rather starve to death.

'This is not a — a — social call, Mr Grant. It's a sort of business matter.' She stood with her hands on her hips, knowing she looked truculent and determined not to soften. This smooth operator, this snake-in-the-grass, this insensitive boor — she would confront him and get an explanation.

He gave her a sideways look. The tone of her voice had got to him. 'Well,' he drawled, 'if you don't mind, we'll go around the back — this door

59

is bolted from the inside.' And he walked jauntily to where a paved path led to the back of the house, through knee-high weeds.

She thumped after him. He had somehow got the upper hand already — she hadn't anticipated this domestic scene. But then, she hadn't anticipated anything much. She had just wanted to confront him and make him feel a bit small. Minuscule if possible.

But now he was juggling with a key, trying to open the kitchen door. Automatically, she held out her hands to take the takeaway cartons and with an ingenuous smile, he handed them over.

Once inside, he turned the food into a pottery casserole, placed it in the microwave and pressed 'Reheat'. And all the time, his frowning concentration was on the job in hand — she might have been several kilometres away.

'Mr Grant — ' she started, standing stiffly by the door.

'Now, before we get down to

business, how about a drink?' he asked smoothly.

'Mr Grant,' she spluttered, 'this is a business call and I don't want a drink.' She heard her voice rising shrilly. Darn it, how does he manage to needle me so easily?

'I see. Well, you don't mind if I — ?' He raised his dark eyebrows in query and then shrugged and turned towards the dresser that doubled as a side-board. She stood fuming, while he poured a small gin, opened the fridge door, lifted out a bottle of tonic water, topped up the gin and then replaced the bottle.

Finally, he turned around, raised the glass to her in a mocking toast and took a sip. 'Now — what's the problem?' he asked kindly.

Somehow, maddeningly, he had made her feel like a child. 'About the theatre — ' she started.

There was a loud beep from the oven. He gave her an apologetic look, put down his drink and lifted out the casserole. As he removed the lid, a cloud of fragrant steam wafted to her quivering nose. It was almost unbearable.

'Look, I rather over-ordered — why don't you join me?'

'No, *thank* you!' she answered tightly and remained standing while he reached for a plate and started to spoon out the sweet-and-sour pork and the fried rice. Great gusts of tantalizing aromas engulfed her.

'You don't mind if I start, do you?' He clearly didn't expect an answer as he started to eat with two ivory chopsticks. 'At least take a seat. You make me nervous hovering like that.'

'Too bad — I'm more comfortable standing.'

He shrugged again and picked up a chunk of carrot adroitly. She took a quick look at the top of the dark head, hair curling crisply around the top of his ears. She'd rather be facing him over a desk. She took a deep breath.

'The theatre — I understand you've bought it.'

'To demolish,' he answered between mouthfuls. 'Are you sure you won't join me? This is delicious.'

She ignored the last comments. 'Why the hell didn't you tell me?'

'You didn't ask me.'

'How could I ask you when I had no idea — '

'You mean, you didn't know anything about it?'

'Nothing — nothing at all. You heard me talking to Hamish about having rocks delivered and — '

'Had no idea where they were being delivered, dear girl.' He took a mouthful of steaming rice.

'Don't 'dear girl' me!' This was too much — high-handed actions were bad enough, but that patronizing manner . . . 'Listen, Mr Grant! I don't know why you've decided to descend in such a magnificent way on this town, but you can't necessarily buy acceptance by throwing money everywhere. We've seen city-based farmers before around here. A good tax lurk, I believe, to invest in acres and livestock and buy up chunks of land to develop, but that's not necessarily progress. I suppose you'll be bulldozing indiscriminately to put up your factory — and never mind the people you've turfed out of their houses.' She was annoyed to hear her voice getting even more shrill.

He had continued to eat while her accusations echoed in the kitchen. It was dark outside now and she had an odd feeling the two of them were in a remote place, far from the rest of humanity. Yet only half-a-kilometre along the road Hamish would be settling down in front of his TV and a kilometre or so further on, the little town would be humming — as far as Ashley ever hummed. No rehearsal tonight but there was a screening of an up-to-date musical — she couldn't remember the title.

Now he chased the last piece of juicy meat around the plate with the chopsticks, concentrating with infinite care on the job in hand.

Finally, he stood up and took the empty plate to the sink beneath the window. Then he turned around and she shivered a little at the expression on his face. Gone was the amiable, gentle-eyed fellow who had caught her in his arms when she had stumbled on the path behind the house.

Instead, his face had lines she'd not noticed before and his eyes were hard as brown gemstones. Even his lips seemed to have thinned as he snapped out: 'Listen to me, Miss Holier-Than-Thou Jensen!'

He pushed her into a kitchen chair with one strong hand and taking another chair, he twirled it quickly and sat with one leg each side, while he leant on its back. His face was on a level with hers and his eyes bored into hers with an intensity that was frightening.

'I think it's time to enlighten you about a few things — although why

I should, I don't know.' He paused for a moment, as if to decide how to continue. 'I'm not into tax lurks, as you put it. But I want my money to work for me. Fourteen years ago, my life was turned upside down and my plans were shattered. I was to train as a veterinarian but my father was cheated by his business partner and the firm had to go into receivership. It was an old family business and it hit him badly. It — ' A shadow crossed his face and his mouth was grim as he continued. 'It killed him, it nearly killed my mother and I had to go to work to support both of us.'

'I'm sorry,' she stammered. Then she took a deep breath. 'But that's got nothing to do with what I'm saying.' She gulped and started again.

'You're seeing the town as a — an investment and nothing more. The hall, the old houses behind it, the workmen's cottages by the river — they're all coming down in the name of progress, right?' She stood up and gripped the back of the chair with white-knuckled hands. Her eyes were flashing.

'Well, I don't call it progress! There'll be no entertainment to speak of for the teenagers, and the old people in some of those houses will have to go into hostels in the city. They'll hate it! Or are you going to build a casino for entertainment and put up new houses for the old people in the down-market part of the town — where your development plans wouldn't be a good proposition?'

There was silence in the room as they faced each other. Outside, a mopoke owl hooted. Her heart was hammering as she looked at his impassive face, his cold eyes. He was a different person from the gracious host who had taken her on a guided tour earlier in the day, occasionally touching her arm lightly to draw her attention to the best features of the land. And she had gone away thinking beautiful thoughts about him . . . That he was 'reliable as the sunrise'. That he had 'integrity' and he was 'honest' and 'he'd never make a dodgy deal'. And that those dark brown eyes were guileless. How naive can you get, Natalie?

Not that he was necessarily dishonest — but he was a hard-nosed businessman. Without needing to be told she knew he wouldn't make any deal unless he was the winner. There would probably be little thought about what would happen to anyone who got in the way.

Her stomach knotted as she looked at that hard expression and the grim line of his mouth. He was standing now and, like her, gripping the back of the chair.

His voice, when he finally responded to her outburst, was gravelly and low. 'Miss Jensen, you are assuming a great deal — probably from ignorance. The development plans are well thought out and no one will suffer. If you'd looked a bit more carefully at those houses you'd have seen they were little more than hovels. A sentimental attitude to all old buildings is fine — as long as you don't let it overcome your common sense.'

'One of those hovels is my family home and my mother still lives there,' she snapped.

'And the roof needs to be replaced, right? And there's dry rot in some of the walls, right? And since the Council is extending the deep drainage to that part of the town, your mother would have to fork out a great deal of money to get the pipes connected, whether or not she wants to — the septic tanks are health hazards.'

He'd done his homework all right. And what he was saying was true, but in her wound-up state, she didn't want to listen to reason.

Suddenly he swung around and pushed his chair under the table. 'I'm happy to continue with our arrangement for the landscaping, but I suggest you stick to your area of expertise and let me get on with mine. Now, if you don't mind, I need to get some sleep. The workmen are arriving early tomorrow and I have to take a trip to Melbourne later in the day.'

He opened the door leading to the front of the house and clicked on a light. Not exactly the charming host, she thought. When it interferes with his plans, he just throws out the guest.

She stalked after him as he strode along the cheerless corridor and into the cavernous hall. He stopped to turn on more lights and she nearly cannoned into him. He was so close she felt the warmth radiating from him and as her arm shot out to steady herself, she touched his back momentarily.

He swung around and stared at her. She stared back, holding her breath. And what devastated her was that she had *wanted* to touch him. She, Natalie Jensen, who had been betrayed by touch, by having her emotions aroused and then left weeping when Gary casually cheated on her, she had *wanted* to touch him.

Her face flamed under his intense look and she turned her head towards

70

the massive entrance door. He remained staring at her for a moment. Then he slid the bolts on the front door and flung it open. Without another word she thumped out and he closed the door firmly behind her.

She didn't feel any triumph at putting him on the spot — she felt totally dispirited. As she drove slowly and carefully down the drive, the head-lights illuminating the huge eucalypts and shadowy acacias, she blinked away tears. Had she made a fool of herself? He had made her feel like an earnest 'greenie' with tunnel vision.

True, she hadn't looked recently at all the old houses backing onto the hall — but they had the appearance of graciousness and charm, especially her mother's. Her childhood home had made a deep impression on her memories. And she could see it clearly as it was then.

Blue-stone construction, high gables, bull-nose return verandas to keep the sun off the windows and 'iron lace' trimmings on the upright veranda posts. Did the roof leak? Was there dry rot? She knew the septic tanks sometimes caused trouble — she had herself footed the bill a few months ago for the plumber, but — a health hazard? And, OK, the theatre hall itself was no showpiece, but it served a purpose. And he was determined to pull down the lot in a totally indiscriminate way.

And yet — and yet! How could he be so sensitive about his own place? She shook her head, remembering the way in which he had talked about renovating the gazebo and the rose gardens. And of how he had run his hands over the gnarled trunk of the wisteria that draped itself over the covered way. And the cattle he intended to buy — he had become quite lyrical.

A mixture of a man, an amalgam of hard-centred and soft-centred traits — like a box of chocolates! She smiled ruefully to herself. 'And wrapped up in the most beautiful package I've ever seen,' she sighed in the darkness, as she swung the Suzuki into the driveway of her half-house.

Tomorrow she would go to see her mother. How would she be feeling about the disaster that would descend on her? She had coped, somehow, with the divorce and the lack of money, but — dispossession?

★ ★ ★

'Yes, I had heard — but I didn't know it was definite until last week, Natalie.'

'But why on earth didn't you tell me?'

'I didn't want to worry you, dear. And you've been so busy.'

Her mother was, as always, delighted to see her. They sat with cups of coffee on cane rocking chairs on the veranda that dripped with jasmine and honeysuckle and hanging baskets of geraniums.

Suddenly Natalie felt guilty. She

leant over and gave her mother a hug. 'I think it's terrible. This lovely old house — '

'Well . . . ' Mary Jensen hesitated. 'The roof has started to leak and . . . ' Her voice tailed off.

Natalie sat upright, nearly spilling the coffee. Her eyes narrowed. 'And what?'

'Oh, darling, it's probably nothing serious, but I think there's dry rot in the wooden surrounds of the fireplace in the lounge. It seems to be spreading rather quickly.' She looked apologetic. 'And the back veranda is sort of *leaning* . . . '

Natalie sat for a minute or two, digesting the information. So he was right, dammit. He knew more about the state of her family home than she did.

'But Mum,' she finally said, miserably, 'Mum, I can't bear to think of this place being demolished.'

Mary Jensen placed a hand gently on her daughter's arm. 'Natalie, there comes a time when one has to move on. I know how you feel about this house, but honestly, dear, it's become a bit — well — dilapidated. And the garden's getting too much for me, especially now I've got the part-time job at the hospital.'

Her eyes lit up. 'And the new places sound great — compact but not too small and just a little patch of ground that will be enough for growing a few flowers and some herbs.'

'What new places?' Natalie turned startled eyes to her mother.

'The units the developer is going to put up on the other side of the park. Didn't you know? He's going to rush the plans through Council as soon as possible and they'll be ready for occupation before these are knocked down. Oh, it'll be lovely to move into a bright new place where everything works!'

★ ★ ★

Does anyone ever really know anyone, Natalie mused as she drove slowly back to the office. Here I was, agonizing over my mum being turned out of the house I thought she loved — and instead, she can't wait.

Shaking her head, she turned the corner and nearly collided with the blue sports car pulling out. It reversed to the kerb and the engine was turned off.

'I thought I was going to miss you,' Connor said coolly, as he unwound himself from the car.

He looked wonderful — dark hair a bit ruffled, those eyes that could be soft as velvet and hard as steel, that rocky frame that made her want to reach out and touch him. How is it that whatever he wears, he looks like something out of *Vogue-Men*? Probably because that's exactly where it all comes from, she answered darkly.

He opened the door of the Suzuki for her and stood aside as she slid to the ground. 'The workmen have arrived — an army of them — and they know what they have to do. I'm on a flight to Melbourne in just over two hours.' He shot back the cuff of his jacket and looked at his watch.

Then his brown eyes flicked over her cornflower-blue T-shirt and he grinned faintly at the inscription: 'Women, The World's Most Undervalued Resource.' He shook his head. 'Not by me, not by me.'

She felt herself blushing. Why was he here? To apologize for his harsh words? Unlikely, but let's wait and see. I rather fancy the idea of his grovelling.

He quickly banished that thought. 'Not sure when I'll be back, but I wondered what chance there was of your starting work sooner than you'd originally said.'

She raised her eyebrows. 'What's the hurry?' She started to walk up the path. She needed to think quickly. The quotation wasn't ready, but if she had to start ordering the materials, she needed some assurance that —

'I thought I could write out a cheque

now, to show good faith.'

'Without a quotation?'

'I trust you,' he answered with a broad grin.

'That's not very businesslike.'

He followed her inside and shut the door behind him. 'There are times, Natalie, when I fly by the seat of my pants — when intuition plays a large part in my actions. I get the feeling now that, no matter how much you disapprove of me and my — er — machinations, you wouldn't take advantage of my trust.'

He was not grinning now. There was an intense look that brought a flutter deep within her. She knew the look — she'd seen it in other men. Gary had perfected it. It was the look that lingered too long for casual social conversation.

And it was directed at her.

4

Never had a look been more potent. Never had she felt that the look reached right into her psyche, stripping all pretence. Never had she been so willing to match that challenge with one of her own. Now her psyche said: this man is different, this one is part of your life now whether or not you want it.

There was nothing casual, nothing flirtatious about that look. It spelled a message of deep attraction and she responded with a bold look that owed a lot to a wish not to be dominated. Gary had dominated her, disastrously, and that would never happen again.

Connor looked startled for an instant at the challenge in her eyes but then two steps forward brought him up against her. His arms slipped around her back and he held her close. It was the episode at the theatre hall, when she'd first met him, all over again. But this time he made no move to kiss her. He stood as if undecided, his eyes wandering over her face while she stood quivering.

Then he spoke in a low voice, his lips barely moving. 'No woman looks at me like that and gets away with it. You, Natalie Jensen, need taking down a peg or two — you are too high and mighty for your own good.'

Only then, in a deliberate and unhurried movement, did he lower his head.

It was total sensation, frightening in its overwhelming power. Natalie closed her eyes but imprinted on her mind was the image of his face. His lips were warm and soft, their contours moulding themselves to hers with firmness and a demand that couldn't be ignored. Her hands fluttered at her sides but then he released his grip a fraction, as if he knew what she wanted. So she was able to hold him in return, sliding her hands up, over the smooth surface of the linen jacket, feeling the hard muscles of his back, knotted now as he clasped her to him.

The kiss settled it. A woman would die for that, she thought hazily.

Heavy clumping footsteps along the path — and they sprang apart. She was gasping for breath and she felt a bright spot of burning colour on each cheek. She nervously pushed her hair behind her ears as Hamish pushed open the door and pulled up short at the sight of them.

She would never know how Connor had managed to reach into an inner pocket, produce a cheque-book and a pen and be bent over the desk, busily scribbling, by the time the door opened.

Why? Why didn't he want to be seen holding her? Not that she wasn't relieved. She didn't want Hamish — or anyone else, for that matter — to witness that scene. To witness her total confusion at what had happened.

What had she done? She had

responded with a need she wouldn't even acknowledge — but the shock of Hamish's entry had been a hefty splash of cold water, returning her to sanity.

'There!' Connor's bland manner calmed her to some extent. He handed Natalie the cheque and gave them both a sweeping grin. 'That should do to start with. Can you begin right away?'

Natalie glanced at the amount and almost keeled over. 'This is far too much for a deposit.'

But Connor was putting away the cheque book and moving towards the door. 'Can't stop now, or I won't make the plane.'

A cool nod to both of them and he was through the door and into the car.

She watched him drive away, conscious of her still-rapid breathing. But Hamish obviously hadn't been aware of anything. He talked about the moss rocks outside the hall — they'd have to be moved again now that the hall was to go, right? 'I'll get on to the supplier and rent the crane for a day, yes? Might as well load them up and get them out to Seymour Rise. From what you said, we'll be needing some out there.'

He started to talk about the need for extra labour — he would take a trip into Gawler today and see what the Employment Service could do.

Natalie agreed dazedly with his proposals. Yes, that would be fine, Hamish, go ahead. How many workmen did he think they'd need for the initial work and for how long? She carried on a sensible and thoughtful conversation until Hamish clumped out again.

Then she collapsed onto the stool, heart still thumping, hands damp with perspiration, and stared for a good five minutes at Kew Gardens' Conservatory on the wall. What was happening to her?

How long had it been since Connor Grant walked into her life? Less than a week? Three years ago she had put men out of her life. She had faced Gary across the kitchen table and yelled at him like a shrew — and it had felt good. It had had a cathartic effect, ridding her of the misery of weeks of slow realization that all was not well. Of hearing whispers of gossip at rehearsals, of wondering why people whom she'd never counted as her friends were looking at her oddly and with a sympathetic flicker in their eyes. Of having Gary evasive and sly and of not being able to put a finger on the trouble.

Until one afternoon, when she'd made a snap decision to call on Rosemary, an old school friend who lived in the next town. And walking in, as she always did, with a cheery 'Yoo-hoo!' and stopping dead in her tracks at the sight of two people hastily donning their clothes in the lounge room. And she hadn't been aware Gary and Rosemary had even known each other.

In a way it had been a relief. Uncertainty had been hard to bear.

Certainty was a slap in the face, painful but definite. She could do something positive. And she had. She had collected her things and moved out of the little cottage where they had set up house, rapturously and trustingly, several months before.

She had built a shell around herself — not sternly or drearily, because that was not her way, but with an apparent flippancy and humour towards the treachery of the opposite sex. And she had issued an implicit challenge to all and sundry that no one, but no one, was going to fool her again.

Because fool her he had. She discovered that Gary had started seeing Rosemary less than a month after Natalie and he had moved into the cottage. 'He just can't help himself, Natalie,' said her friend with an embarrassed giggle. And Natalie, wounded and disenchanted, had turned away.

She shook herself and blinked and,

unintentionally, her chin came up in a determined gesture of defiance. Gary was part of her past and well-lost.

Get back to work, banish this one too and don't waste any more time thinking of those eyes, that mouth and that dishy frame. He is just another man and treacherous to boot.

★ ★ ★

'Great just great, Natalie! If you ever want to change careers, you'd better take up stage production.' The well-wishers surrounded her on the stage, the last-night party in full swing.

All her friends were there, and many others she'd never seen before. Clive and his smiling wife and their neighbours had come in a party. Her own mother, with some other nurses from the hospital were in a group. And watching her from the hall, an impassive Connor, who slowly raised his hand in a solemn salute, before he turned away and melted into the departing crowd.

She felt a momentary stab of disappointment. She'd have liked him to join in the party. But he knew hardly anyone, she realized. Yet, with his confidence, she was surprised he hadn't taken the opportunity to mix a bit, to get to know some of the people in Ashley. After all, he'd soon be a well-known figure, she reflected, with all that development going on. *And* the lord of the manor. She grinned to herself and turned to Sandra, who was jumping up and down at her elbow.

'Natalie, meet Uncle Jeremy.'

Uncle Jeremy was large and, thought Natalie, appropriately avuncular. He was jolly, and he'd spent a pleasant evening watching his favourite niece perform pleasantly, but he wasn't writing out any contracts. Natalie was enough of a realist to know that amateur dramatics were just that — amateur. No matter how dedicated the cast members were and how well they were directed, there was a sizeable gap between them and professional actors.

Uncle Jeremy talked with her for a while, congratulating her on the production and then he drifted away and to his car, to make the journey to Adelaide where he had business the next day.

Gradually the numbers thinned and, at three o'clock, Natalie was left to clear up the place.

'Leave it until the morning, Nat,' said Hamish, taking a bowl of limp salad out of her hands. 'You've done enough this week. Some of the others should've stayed behind to help. You'll be a cot-case if you don't get some sleep.'

He'd been in the auditorium at the end of one row, she'd noticed, as she peeped through the curtains when the hall was filling. But when she'd glanced out again to see how the audience was reacting to one of the dramatic earlier scenes, she'd seen that his eyes were on a self-possessed, dark-haired girl in the row in front.

So that's Marie, Natalie had thought. That's the one who's giving him a hard time, is it? And he has eyes for nothing and no one else. She'd swallowed hard. Such devotion was worthy of more than indifference. Such devotion was hard to find, she thought.

And then her gaze had landed on the dark face of Connor Grant. In one of the best seats, his arms folded across his chest, he was following the stage action closely. Her heart had slammed into her ribs and her treacherous thoughts said: he'd inspire devotion.

She'd turned away from the peep-hole, horrified at her barely-acknowledged conclusion. What was she thinking about? And she'd returned to her job of watching every move of the actors.

Now she made a rueful face as she looked around at the post-party chaos. 'Yep. You're right, Hamish. But I just want to say goodbye to the old place before it gets clobbered. You go home.'

He looked at her sympathetically. 'There'll be somewhere else, you'll see. Somewhere you can put on more plays.'

'I expect so. But this place, tatty though it is — I'm — I'm — well, fond of it.' To her, it was the end of an era. Change was in the air, and she wasn't sure she liked the idea all that much.

'If I go, promise me you'll leave all the mess?'

She promised, and Hamish thumped out to his truck and drove off.

She wandered around, closing windows, making sure the pie-warming oven was off, and the remaining milk was in the fridge. Then she walked slowly out of the front door, locking it behind her.

Sitting for a moment in her car, she looked back. Hamish had removed the moss rocks the week before and now the place was desolate. She would miss the fun, the camaraderie, the excitement of putting on a production.

She would not come this way again, she decided. She'd keep well away so as not to see the demolition work. Sighing, she reached for the ignition.

Then she stopped, her hand in midair. A low-slung car was cruising slowly down the road, a dark, bearded face just showing on the driver's side, staring at the hall. The car stopped for a second, while the driver rolled down the window and peered more closely.

Natalie, her car hidden under the heavy branches of an overhanging acacia, sat motionless. As she watched, the window was slowly wound up and the car moved on. And in the still night air, she heard Connor Grant roaring back on the road to Romney Plains.

★ ★ ★

'What do you think, Hamish? This has to go but I could suggest it's reinstated down there, behind the ballroom.'

Hamish looked doubtfully at the swimming pool and shook his head.

'Don't think we should get too much involved, Nat. I know it's got to fit in with the aspect from the house — and it won't be obtrusive there. But we'd better get an engineer in, to look at the drainage. It may be that some of that plumbing can be rescued — gonna be a helluva waste otherwise.'

Natalie nibbled at her bottom lip. At the moment the question of the pool was holding everything up. The mass of water had to be removed but the manner in which that happened had to be carefully planned. She'd like to be consulting Connor over all sorts of things but he seemed to be spending a great deal of time in Melbourne. He had put his house there on the market and apparently he was organizing to transfer most of his work to Adelaide, retaining only a small office in Melbourne.

She'd seen very little of him since the final night of the play, two weeks before. He'd called at the office once and on another occasion he'd quietly walked up behind her when she was taking photographs of the vista from the top of the terraces.

She had carefully avoided the topic of the demolition. The whole of the development plan was a *fait accompli* so what was the point of getting into arguments or recriminations? But it rankled with her.

Of equal irritation was the fact of his frequent absences at the initial stages of the landscaping. Later on, it wouldn't be so vital, but now she needed to point out how stages had to follow logically one after another — and a phone call wouldn't do.

When she'd mentioned that to Hamish, he had looked knowingly at her. 'No, you need him to be around, don't you?' When she'd glared at him, he'd added hastily, 'So that he can see exactly what you mean, right?' And she had turned away, annoyed at Hamish's astute observations.

She had told Connor that progress could be held up if she couldn't ask his opinion at various stages, and he had said airily, 'Oh, I'm sure you can make most decisions satisfactorily without me, Natalie. I just want the place to look cared-for and for the vegetation to be right for the climate and the topography. Oh, and the view to Mount Memory — that's pretty terrific, yes? Except that there are some odd-looking trees here and there. They seem to be the wrong height or something. I don't know exactly why, but they look — wrong.'

Natalie was pleased about that. He may have been a bit vague about the technicalities of landscaping, but he could recognize that scale and proportion played a large part in the resultant look of the place. And he was right. The trees he had pointed out had been haphazardly planted, with no apparent theme or unity. What's more, they were exotics and would require huge amounts of water all year round. They would have to come out.

But now the pool remained the

biggest problem. 'I suppose he wants a pool?' asked Hamish. 'It would be heaps easier if we could just gently drain away the water and bulldoze the site.'

'Yep. I want it.'

Natalie jumped at the sound of the deep voice. She wished fervently that he would cough or sing or generally make some noise as he walked around. She and Hamish might have been making uncomplimentary remarks about him, she thought, grinning to herself. But she knew it was unintentional; he was just light on his feet — surprising for such a large man.

She hadn't even known he was in South Australia. He'd gone to Melbourne the previous week to arrange for his furniture to be transported across. The painters and plumbers and carpenters had worked like Trojans and in a month the place had been transformed. And now it was ready for habitation and looking elegant and dignified like a grand duchess with the skirts of the partially-restored garden around her.

He looked terrific, she decided. The inevitable moleskins with a crisp shirt tucked in and the Gucci loafers. His beard, full-grown, was black and bushy but trimmed to a neat shape. His eyes, narrowed slightly in the strong late-summer sun, looked her up and down and then slid towards Hamish. 'I swim every day if I can — in fact, I want the new one to be larger. But this,' he jerked his head towards the murky depths of the pool, 'will soon be gone — I've got a contract signed. And yes, I agree, it'll be behind the — er — ballroom.'

Now why did he hesitate over the word 'ballroom'? Natalie frowned. There had been workmen all over the place, and some were even now beavering away in there. Did he feel the idea of a ballroom was a bit — effeminate?

Hamish muttered something about

moving the front-end loader and ambled off.

Connor sat on the top step by the pool, stretching his legs in front of him. 'I want to talk to you, Natalie.'

She looked at him out of the corner of her eyes. There was adequate space next to him on the step but she didn't want to sit there — it was too close. But he looked up at her with a grin, a challenging grin that infuriated her. She realized she'd look silly if she insisted on sitting elsewhere in a prim fashion. Almost as if she were *afraid* to sit next to him.

And that was the truth, she knew, as she perched on the step as far away as possible — a difficult feat, when the step was only about a metre wide — and stretched out her own, jean-clad legs.

He grinned again, knowingly this time, and looked pointedly at the space between them. 'Scared?' he asked in a low voice.

She almost spluttered with indignation.

'Of course I'm not scared — what is there to be scared about?' And an inner voice supplied the answer. You're scared all right, because he's been dominating your thoughts since he walked into the hall that night and that is what no other man has done since Gary.

He looked deep into her eyes. 'Your eyes,' he said slowly, 'remind me of stormy seas and — '

'Connor Grant,' she interrupted sharply and a little too loudly, 'I thought you wanted to talk to me about the plans.'

'I just said I wanted to talk to you,' he said mildly.

They sat in silence for a few moments. The grinding noise of Hamish repositioning his front-end loader came to them from behind the ballroom. And overhead, there was a breathtaking glimpse of rosy-breasted galahs as a flock flew over and then disappeared behind one of the huge eucalypts.

'Something's happened to you, Natalie

— something that makes you hostile and a little — uh — prickly.' Connor looked ahead with an impassive face.

She hesitated before responding. 'Lots of things happen to people in their lives that leave them a — a little — wary.'

Another silence, while he appeared to digest her comment. Then, 'It's more than wariness, Natalie. It goes far deeper than that.'

Why should she unburden her heart to him? He was just showing an intrusive curiosity, teasing her a little perhaps. She brushed an imaginary leaf from her jeans. 'I really don't see where this conversation is leading. Are you a frustrated social worker or something?'

He laughed. 'No, I don't intend to try to counsel you. It's just that I'd like our professional relationship to be a bit more relaxed and friendly.'

She stiffened. 'Do you have any complaints?'

'No, of course not. Everything's going very well indeed. But I'd like it very much if we could, well, see more of each other.' He grinned. 'Let me rephrase that. I'd like to see you away from here and talk about things other than landscaping.'

Again, that fear in her heart — a fear of being fooled by a plausible and smooth-spoken male — made her speak more harshly than she intended.

'Connor, I have a great deal to do — not just on your place but for other projects. I think it would be better if we were to keep the relationship on a professional level. And now,' she added, standing hurriedly and starting to descend the steps, 'I must see Hamish about some levelling . . .'

She wasn't running away, she told herself. There was work to be done. There was silence behind her but as she reached the bottom of the steps and skirted the house she knew, without looking, that two sombre brown eyes were watching her every move. The knowledge made her breathless.

There were three huge pantechnicons

pulled up on the gravel in front of the house. As she arrived, four workmen were gently easing an ornate side-board down one of the ramps. In the dim interior of the van, she glimpsed more pieces, some still carefully draped with large cloths and secured by ropes and some standing ready to be unloaded.

And through the now-shining windows she could see that the place was slowly filling up. She surreptitiously peeped in one or two of the windows and gave a low whistle. She wasn't all that knowledgeable about antique furniture, but she knew that this was the real McCoy. It was good stuff, with a patina of age and loving care. And it was standing on the most beautiful collection of Persian and Chinese rugs that she'd ever seen. The house would be a showpiece, yet there was a comfortable air to the rooms. It was all immensely livable. And worth, without doubt, a fortune.

As she walked towards the noise of the hidden front-end loader, she could see a trade van with the name of a security firm on the side panel. Connor was taking no chances — the place was obviously being wired up — or whatever it was that security firms did to protect a house and its contents.

But despite all the activity, Natalie couldn't get the thought of Connor's words out of her mind. She wandered down to the first terrace, absent-mindedly snapping off a dead rose here, a spray of withered blossoms there. What had he said? ' — more relaxed and friendly . . . and talk about things other than landscaping.' What things? She kicked at a stone with her desert boot. The weather?

No, Natalie, her common sense told her, not the weather. There was something in that look he gave her that reminded Natalie of the occasion in her office, just before he had kissed her. And that was a long, long way from matters meteorological, she thought, with a flutter deep inside her. It was an invitation — a blatant invitation to put their relationship on an intimate footing, to seek out the inner thoughts and feelings of two people who are mutually attracted.

Mutually? She leant against the trunk of an overhanging acacia, her heart thumping. I haven't got the time for this. Life is too full as it is. I haven't got room for a new experience, not now. Maybe not ever. Her thoughts became a little panicky. I don't want to probe the reasons for my feelings, let alone have him probe. And I don't want to be diverted from my goals.

Suddenly her goals were a lifeline — a lifeline to sanity. She pushed herself away from the tree and trudged back towards the house. If she needed anything at this very moment, it was the solid, common-sense approach of Hamish.

But as she rounded the corner of the house again, her eyes flew to the top of the steps by the swimming pool. And there, in the same relaxed, sprawling posture as when she'd left him, Connor Grant was staring down, his dark eyes looking for all the world as if he had been waiting for her to reappear.

5

'I'm sure you can make most decisions satisfactorily without me, Natalie,' he'd said. Most of them, yes. But now she was stumped.

Connor Grant had flown to Melbourne again but, in any case, he probably couldn't help her on this one. The vista to Mount Memory was worrying her. OK, for most people it would be a pretty view. But for her, it could be a breathtaking and deeply satisfying prospect. And for Connor, too, she knew. He had a vision for that sweep of terraces down to the flat paddocks, framed by carefully placed trees. It might not be necessary to replant — with the exotics removed, it could be perfect.

But she needed to talk to Kurt. He had been her mentor in the earlier days. Nowadays, he put all his energy into his magnificent garden in one of the leafier suburbs of Adelaide and his landscaping business had been sold. But she would be eternally grateful for his recognition of the fact that she had the necessary ability and vision to go ahead on her own and not just as one of his helpers.

There was a menacing feel to the humidity as she threw the packed grip and her bulging briefcase into the back of the Suzuki. She would take all her plans and some photos to show Kurt, and she had included photos of recent landscaping projects she and Hamish had carried out. He'd like to see how she was progressing.

On the western horizon, dark, fast-moving clouds were massing. Natalie knocked on Hamish's front door. 'Sorry to do this to you at six o'clock on a Saturday morning,' she remarked as he appeared, tousle-haired and sleepy-eyed. 'But I've decided to take a trip to Adelaide to see Kurt. I need some advice and he can give me a good, objective viewpoint.'

He mumbled about some coffee and she stepped inside. Over hot, steamy cups they talked.

There had been no news as yet from the Hospital Board, but she felt hopeful about the tender. It was just as well, she said, that they weren't in too much of a hurry. 'It'll give us more time to spend on Seymour Rise. And Mrs Travers' fountain — it needs checking, Hamish. The pump was playing up yesterday and her relatives are due next week. Could you pop over there today and see what's wrong?'

'No worries, Nat,' said Hamish with a huge yawn. 'The weather's looking daggy — we'll get a cool change soon, for sure.' There was a sudden rattling gust of rain against the window. 'She'll have all the trickling water she wants if we get much of that.'

Natalie laughed and dabbed at her forehead with her handkerchief. 'You should have given me iced coffee, Hamish. It's early still, but it's going to be a stinker today. Wish I had air-conditioning in the Suzuki.'

'Listen, Nat, it's not my department, but I'm not sure your friend Kurt is going to be much help without coming here and having a look at the place. It's hard to explain a view!'

She nibbled at her bottom lip. 'I've got some photos — but, yes, I need more. There's no way Kurt can get up here — ' She looked at the wall clock in Hamish's kitchen. 'I'll dash up there now, before I leave.' She laughed as she stood up. 'I must get to Adelaide by nine or I won't have enough time to browse around the stores.'

'Buying up big, eh? Lots of new clothes?' asked Hamish with a grin, as he opened the front door for her.

'Just a few, Hamish. Getting a bit sick of jeans and shirt all the time. Need to remind myself I'm a girl, occasionally.'

'Oh, I don't think anyone would have any doubt about that. Certainly not

Connor Grant!' And Hamish closed the door quickly.

If he doesn't stop making innuendoes like that, she thought, driving in at the gates of Seymour Rise, I won't give him that rise he really deserves. The firm may be called Jensen and MacIntyre but that was because it had a ring to it — people remembered the double name easily. But Hamish didn't want to be a partner — not yet, anyway. She'd offered him a partnership but he'd said he needed to get his finances in order first. The cottage renovations had taken all his money and if he was going to be a partner, he'd have to make it worth her while financially, he'd said.

Natalie glanced at the sky as she prepared to step out of the vehicle onto gravel already pooled with rain. Not the best weather for photos but it needed to be done now.

She hesitated for a moment inside the car. It was teeming now and the view to Mount Memory was rapidly becoming grey with the sweeping clouds of heavy rain. There was a sudden flash of lightning and then a deafening clap of thunder. Darn it! She compressed her lips with annoyance. Hamish was right, she needed those photos but they really had to be good.

There was a sudden gap in the clouds and a lessening of the rain and she leapt out. Positioning the camera, she took a photo and jumped back inside to listen to the whirring as the print rolled out. A few seconds later she was looking at a passable image of the view to Mount Memory. Not good enough, she decided.

She sighed. Maybe she'd better forget that browse around the big stores. She'd wait until the rain eased. And as if to mock her, it bucketed down. She felt too vulnerable here — she'd pull up under the portico, where there'd be some protection from the elements, she decided. Never been struck by lightning, but it's an experience I can do without.

Half-an-hour later the gravel was awash. It was powdery-dry underneath from months of near-drought conditions, and the water was taking forever to soak into the concrete-like surface. Every gutter on the big house was overflowing. Leaves in the downpipes, she thought, but at least, after the effort put in by the roofing workers, there won't be any leaking onto his beautiful furniture. He must have spent a great deal of time collecting that, she mused. It was perfect for the old house and she had to admire his style.

She thought for a moment about his style — in all matters. There was, she decided, a style in the way he dressed, the way he moved, even the way in which he went about his business dealings. Reluctantly, she could recognize that. And, said the inner voice, the way he approached women? She'd not seen him with other women but that smooth yet sincere approach that had hooked her was polished with style. Huh!

Another gap in the clouds and she leapt out again. Another photo — that would do it. Kurt would be able to get the idea. And if she put a move on, she might be able to get to Adelaide by eleven. That would still give her a few hours, now that the shopping hours had been extended 'in response to overwhelming demand.' She smiled to herself. Whose demand? Certainly not the shop assistants', who'd really rather have their Saturday afternoons off.

She drove carefully down the driveway, the potholes now filled in but the surface not yet bitumenized. It was sloshy with mud and as she turned the corner by the monster eucalyptus, she gasped.

The creek was flowing. Fed by numerous tributaries, the brown water was roaring down the creek bed that had been dry when she'd driven over the culvert earlier. She must have spent more time sitting in the car than she had realized. Brooding about Connor most of the time, too, she thought with annoyance.

Now the little bridge had more than a foot of water rushing over it and Natalie hesitated. The Suzuki was high on its wheels but the water had a force about it that worried her.

No, she had to do it. She eased the car forward just as a surge of water swept away a partial dam of branches and leaves upstream. She saw the approaching wave just in time and slammed on the brakes before she reached the culvert.

But she was halfway down the slope now and she felt the car sliding sideways in the mud towards the torrent. She flung the gear into reverse but the vehicle was too far gone. The wheels span with a complaining whine from the transmission.

'That, Natalie Jensen, is going to get you nowhere.' She turned off the ignition hurriedly. The car was still gently sliding towards the side of the culvert, but then it stopped, teetering on the edge. Moving carefully, she picked up her grip and her briefcase and the camera and slid along the seat.

Edging herself out, she scrambled back up the slope, slithering on the muddy surface, and collapsed on the higher ground. She turned to look at the Suzuki. It was perched on the edge of the rushing creek, and already the water had reached floor level.

'Natalie, that was not a very clever thing to do,' she told herself shakily. Her hair was plastered to her head and she started to shiver with the feel of sodden clothes. The swirling water seemed to rise with each passing moment. She'd have to get to the other side of the creek quickly or it would be too late. Given the depth of the original creek bed and adding the height of the water, she gauged that the total depth must be about four feet. And the water was crashing along with the force of an angry giant.

'Don't even think about it,' she

muttered. She was strong but she wasn't game to battle with *that*.

Above her head the eucalypts were swaying dangerously in the roaring wind. River Red gums, she noted, with a nasty habit of dropping large boughs. Although she seemed to remember that it was usually *after* the gale was over that they did that. For all that, let's not live dangerously, she thought. I've had enough excitement for one day.

There was nothing for it but to pick herself up and trudge back to the house. Hamish would come and rescue her in the truck, she reasoned. He'd have no trouble with the rising water.

But how would he know? As far as he was concerned, she was on her way to Adelaide. And that was what she had told her mother too. 'Oh, hell!' she muttered, as the house came in sight. 'I'll just have to get to the phone — I'll look a bit of a dill, but pride must be swallowed.' Hamish, she thought ruefully, would never let her forget it.

A phone? The realization of her predicament hit her. The house was empty, wasn't it? The workmen had departed for the weekend and the place was securely locked and, probably, with the security system firmly in place.

She stood under the portico, dripping and feeling intensely sorry for herself. Her jeans were mud to the knee and her boots squelched. Rat's-tails of hair dangled around her face and she started to shiver again in the now-cold wind that gusted around her.

Maybe around the back of the house? She remembered a garden shed. Perhaps she could shelter for a while, until the creek subsided. Thank God she'd remembered to grab her grip — dry, clean clothes would feel wonderful.

First, a reconnaissance. She carefully placed her luggage close to the front door, well away from any splashes. Then she plodded around to the back.

For a moment she thought she was imagining things. The path disappeared into another stream, it seemed. Feeling so wet that it didn't matter any more, she waded through and around to the kitchen entrance. The water was lapping the step. And as she watched, mud and stones clattered down the hill behind her.

The pool! With a horrified gasp, she looked up. The small leak that she and Connor had seen five weeks before, a tiny green give-away in dry surroundings, was bubbling with energy. Even as she gave a cry of alarm, another burst of water tore away more of the surrounding earth.

Natalie took the steps two at a time and pulled up sharply at the top. The pool was brimming, with more water pouring into it from numerous rivulets on the side of the hill. Why wasn't it draining properly? There should have been water gushing out below, keeping the level constant.

She ran down the steps again, to the tangle of pipes she and Hamish had inspected a few days earlier. They were clearly not functional, a general air of decay and rust making it obvious that neglect had prevented them from doing their job. They would be blocked with mud and leaves. She mentally cursed the previous owners.

If only she could open up the drainage, the bulk of the water would pour away harmlessly, across the doomed rose garden and down the back of the ballroom and across the terraces.

Otherwise . . . 'Oh no! Not inside the house!' She was yelling, but it didn't matter. There was no one to hear her. But inside the house, all Connor's antique furniture, standing on exquisite Oriental rugs, a sitting target for the brown, muddy water threatening to pour under the kitchen door.

She whirled around, her eyes searching for something, anything, that she could use. But it was heavy piping — it would need more than a spanner. It would need a steam roller or some other weighty machinery, like a —

Natalie yelped with triumph. The front-end loader! Heavy and a bit ponderous, but capable of breaking pipes as heavy as these, as Hamish had once discovered, to his embarrassment, when he'd breached a mains' pipe in a client's garden. As she ran towards where it was parked, she allowed herself a slight smile at the memory of Hamish, gazing horrified at the geyser that had spouted over his head.

The loader started at once. 'I love you, I love you,' Natalie muttered, patting the control panel as it spluttered into life. She engaged the gear and drove it slowly and carefully around the ballroom and towards the drainage pipes.

In the event, it was a pushover. One rumbling lunge over and back and the pipes broke away with a splintering explosion and a gurgling rush of water cascaded into the rose garden and away.

But it wouldn't be quick enough, she realized. She drove nearer to the house and saw that the water was already seeping in under the kitchen door. Working furiously, she dug the mechanical shovel into the ground outside the door, scooping up mud and stones and had the satisfaction of seeing the muddy water pouring back from the door into the large hole she had gouged.

More backwards and forwards, working to make a deep gully along the back of the house. It was time-consuming work, manipulating the loader carefully in the confined space so as not to damage the walls of the house. She lost sense of time, focusing her thoughts totally on the job. Then, suddenly, it was all over. The water that was still pouring down the hill from the pool gurgled and tumbled safely into the deep ditch she had dug and rushed away to join the rest.

And as she sat on the worn seat of the loader, with the rain pelting on her, the stream from the pool lessened and the breach in the wall showed no further sign of breaking away.

She clambered down and climbed wearily to check the level. The pool was half empty. She gave a huge sigh and then frowned. A rhythmic throbbing noise — a helicopter in this weather?

It appeared from the direction of Adelaide, banking as it approached the flat expanse of paddock below the terraces. She watched, oblivious to the rain which was finally beginning to ease, until the aircraft disappeared from her view in front of the house.

Had someone come to rescue her? But how could they know? Both Hamish and her mother would think she'd be in Adelaide by now.

She trudged down the steps, her desert boots making little fountains as they squeezed out the water from her soggy socks. But then her head came up in alarm. The quiet humming of the plane had suddenly ceased. And before it had ceased there had been a nasty crunching noise.

'Connor! Oh, Connor! Please open your eyes!' She crouched in the cockpit, holding his head in her hands. Above her the rotor blades were twisted at an odd angle and one blade had dug into the earth but, thankfully, the main body of the helicopter looked undamaged.

His face was white under the beard but he was breathing, she ascertained. And then, to her immense relief, he opened his eyes.

He stared at her for a few moments as if he didn't recognize her. Then, 'Natalie?' She gave him a wobbly smile. 'Natalie, what the devil are you doing here?'

'I might ask the same question, Connor Grant,' she answered softly. 'Do you make a habit of this?'

He looked over her shoulder at the rotor blade. 'Oh my God! That'll need more than a pair of pliers to fix.'

How they could be making light of what was potentially a fatal situation,

she would never know. But it was a
form of instant therapy, she decided.
So as not to let the situation overwhelm
them.

'I was fine — nearly touched down
— until there was a sudden gust
of wind — I haven't had enough
experience . . . ' His voice tailed off
wearily. 'They told me to take it gently
for a while, but — '

' — but you knew better, didn't
you?' Her voice was gentle, to take
away the implied criticism. 'Can you
move all your joints?'

Still inside the cockpit, he flexed his
arms and legs. 'They seem OK, but I
guess there'll be a few bruises.' She
jumped down to the ground as he
edged himself out. 'Ouch, I guessed
right.'

But the colour was coming back
into his face and he was able to
reach inside and pull out a suitcase
and his briefcase. With a last wincing
look at the rotors, he turned with her
towards the house. Buffeted by the

wind, and a few stray, pelting showers, they struggled across the paddock.

Neither of them spoke — it was too difficult to make themselves heard over the roaring of the wind and the crashing of the boughs over their heads. He led the way around the back of the house and pulled up with a shout of surprise.

'What on earth — ?' He turned to her. 'What's been happening?'

Choosing her words carefully, playing it down a bit, she explained. And all the time, he stood transfixed, his eyes shooting from her to the loader, then back to her face, then up the hill to the pool surrounds.

'I'm — er — sorry about the rose garden,' she said in the end. 'Most of the bushes must be on their way to Mount Memory by now.'

He put down his case and reached for her. 'You did all that for me? In the pouring rain? By yourself?' He held her close and shook his head wonderingly. 'What a woman!'

Suddenly it was all too much. The shocks of the past two hours, the episode in the Suzuki, the sight of the water pouring down the hill, struggling with the loader and then, to crown it all, Connor's still, white face in the helicopter — it finally hit her and she burst into tears.

'Oh, Natalie, my dear! You poor girl!' For a full minute he held her close, while she sobbed into his wet clothes. Then he gave her a final hug and held her at arm's length. 'If I wasn't afraid I might drop you, in my state of health, I'd carry you inside. As it is,' and he fished in his pocket for the key, 'you are going to get into some dry clothes and have a hot drink just as soon as it can be organized.'

He unlocked the kitchen door and, before stepping inside, he pulled out a small remote-control from his briefcase and pressed a button. 'We'd better inactivate the security system or the whole neighbourhood will come running, including the police.'

Natalie, trembling slightly from the remembered feel of his arms around her and his affectionate words, made her way through the house to get her luggage. As she went, she stared at the transformed hall, the walls now fresh with pastel-blue paint, the staircase banisters gleaming and the stairs covered with a runner of Persian carpet. Gilt-framed mirrors were strategically hung over half-round rosewood tables in the hall and, in pride of place, a large Oriental rug, its jewel colours glowing in the half-light.

She could see glimpses of the rooms each side of the hall, furnished now, and giving an opulent welcome that had been missing when she had first seen the place — how many weeks ago? Weeks in which she had felt herself being drawn, unwillingly but inexorably, towards its owner. She could hear him now, clattering away in the brightly-lit kitchen.

Shivering at the thought of what

would have happened to all this if she hadn't been there in time, she scooped up her luggage and went back to Connor.

★ ★ ★

'I think,' Connor said slowly, 'that it's going to be a little while before you become mobile again.'

The huge tree trunk lay, right-angled across the drive, its roots half-clear of a gaping hole in the leaf-covered ground, its upper branches smashed against another eucalyptus on the opposite side. It could not have fallen more neatly, thought Natalie. Beyond, still dangerously close to the raging water, her little car looked forlorn, abandoned.

They had trudged together from the house, warmed by cups of fragrant coffee and both with dry clothes. The rain had stopped, but it would be a long time before the creek subsided completely. It was still being fed by a multitude of tributaries upstream.

When she had told him what had happened, his eyes had widened. 'You've had quite a day, haven't you?' Then he had suggested that the loader would probably be able to pull the Suzuki back to safety. But now he shook his head. 'Even that piece of machinery can't shift a trunk like that. It'll need a full-sized bulldozer.'

So they trudged back again. And in the warm kitchen he lifted the phone. 'Dead,' he muttered, replacing the receiver. 'That probably wasn't the only tree that came down.'

They stared at each other as realization of their predicament hit them. Then his face slowly creased into a smile.

'So! What do we do now?' He seemed to be enjoying the situation enormously. 'The chopper's kaput until I can get someone up from Adelaide. Your car is out of reach. We can't summon help by phone. Is anyone likely to come looking for you?'

Reluctantly she answered: 'No. Not until Monday.'

'Depending on how things work out — up to two whole days in my sole company. Will you be able to stand it?'

6

She looked at him with wide eyes, her stomach contracting. Then she compressed her lips, refusing to answer. His eyes were teasing her now, their brown depths warm and amused. He seemed to have recovered completely from the helicopter crash. He was back to his normal, confident self and enjoying the potent situation. She turned away to look out of the window. In circumstances like these, how was she to remain aloof and professional? And just to complicate matters, her stomach rumbled.

'Food!' he remarked thoughtfully. 'Are we going to be able to eat?'

'I sincerely hope so — I don't fancy the life of a hunter and gatherer, even for a weekend.'

He flung open the door of the freezer attached to the fridge and his eyes narrowed as he surveyed the contents. 'I must have had a premonition. There's steak and a chicken and some pizzas and — ' He turned back to her with a huge grin. 'We could shack up here for days and days.'

'The words 'shack up' hardly fit the surroundings,' she said drily. And, privately, she didn't like the connotations of the expression.

'Or the situation, I suppose,' he responded softly.

He was deliberately trying to embarrass her — and he was almost succeeding. But no, Connor Grant, there is no way I am going to let you know how your words affect me. Her chin came up.

'You're dead right! Look, if I'm to be your guest for the weekend, albeit unwillingly, the least you can do is to get some food cooked before I starve to death. It's nearly three o'clock and all I've had today is two cups of coffee.'

He gave her one last lingering look and turned back to the freezer. 'Yes, there needs to be some thawing out if the weekend is not to be a disaster,' he said innocently.

★ ★ ★

'Come and see what's been done to the house,' Connor said.

The chicken had been thawed in the microwave and was now gently roasting on sensor-cook. With a raid on a cupboard-full of tinned food for vegetables to accompany it, there would be a meal in less than an hour. She had to hand it to him, he'd done a terrific job of stocking up the kitchen.

So he gave her a conducted tour of the rooms. First the elegant and slightly sombre dining-room, with its ten-seater cedar table and matching chairs, their wine-coloured brocade seats glowing in the muted light.

'I want to entertain, using a catering service,' he said, noting her raised eyebrows. 'And, who knows, one day the whole family may sit at it.' There was a faint smile playing around his lips.

The whole family? There had been no occasion for him to mention his family before. She tried to remember whether he'd ever said 'we' or 'our' but if he had, she'd never noticed. He'd make a lovely dad, she thought fleetingly. And husband? Her mind skittered away from that question. The thought of an intimate life with Connor Grant brought a shiver to her limbs and she turned to the huge cedar sideboard that she'd seen being unloaded and which now dominated one wall.

'May I?' she asked, her hand on one of the cupboard doors.

'Go ahead.'

It was a beautiful piece of furniture, every door and drawer lined with maple and all in spotless condition. 'I had to have it thoroughly stripped and polished,' he said, running his hand over the softly-gleaming surface. 'You wouldn't recognize it if you'd seen it in the showroom. One of those times when one needs to look under the surface and see the gold beneath the dross, you might say. A bit like me, I suppose,' he added deprecatingly, but with a smile that indicated that he was only half-serious.

She looked at him from the corners of her green eyes. 'Dross? Not like you to put yourself down, is it?'

'I try to do it before other people do, Natalie. It tends to disarm them.' He perched on the edge of the table, his arms folded. 'And there are times when I know that what I'm doing is right, even if other people condemn me for it.'

So he wanted to reopen that topic, did he? She strolled over to the window, her hands in the pockets of her jeans, and looked at the leaden sky. 'Like me, you mean?'

'You certainly spoke your mind that day. Tell me, Natalie, do you still feel resentful of my plans to improve parts of the town?'

'When people talk about 'improvements' they are mostly using subjective measurements.' She turned around to face him, her chin only very slightly jutting.

'I agree. But there is nothing in what I am doing that will disadvantage anyone, right?'

'Wrong! There will no longer be a theatre hall for entertainment and there are people being turned out of their houses, where they've lived all their lives — '

His face showed impatience as he interrupted her. 'Have you looked into the details of the development plan, Natalie?'

'How could I?'

'Very easily. It's on display at the Council offices.'

She mentally kicked herself. He was right. She should have known that anything as far-reaching as that would attract interest even if an environmental impact statement weren't necessary.

'Those people are being paid the

market value of their houses and in all cases that will give them considerably more than is needed to buy one of the units that are being offered.'

She tucked a tendril of hair behind each ear. 'There's such a thing as sentiment, but I don't suppose you would worry about that, let alone be prepared to put a cash value on it.' Her voice was getting louder and she felt annoyed that she had allowed herself to be drawn into an argument again over a matter where they could never see eye-to-eye.

He walked slowly towards her, his eyes on her face. When he spoke, his voice had a soft, intimate quality to it that made her shiver. 'Sentiment is of prime importance to me, Natalie. If you think there is none of that in my makeup, then you are simply looking at the exterior. The dross, you might say.'

She held her breath. There was only a few centimetres between them. For a moment, confident dark-brown eyes looked deep into frightened sea-green eyes. For frightened she was. Frightened of the effect of his closeness on her heartbeat, frightened of how she would react if he touched her.

Outside, some kookaburras were cackling their evening, joy-of-living song and the sky was darkening all the time, even though it would be several hours to nightfall. And inside, a silence that was almost tangible as they stared at each other.

Then he turned abruptly. 'Now the other rooms . . .'

She breathed again, and followed him as he made his way towards the rest of the house. His shoulders were broad and strong under the cotton-knit shirt but he moved lightly, in an athletic way. And she had to fight an urge to walk up behind him and put her arms around that sturdy frame.

Get a hold on yourself, Natalie, she thought as he opened the door to the drawing-room and clicked on some low, softly-lit lamps. Just because he has nice eyes and an endearing habit of making you feel fragile and feminine, it doesn't mean he would welcome a closer relationship. The hug outside the kitchen door was just a paternalistic reaction to your tears.

And the close encounter in her office, six weeks ago? There was nothing paternalistic about that. Oh shut up, she told herself, walking into the spacious room.

'I'm still looking for the right sort of chandelier,' he murmured, looking up. 'In the meantime, I like the soft lights.' It was all attractive — and more. He had been careful not to overload the rooms. There was no danger of the place looking like a furniture showroom and he had been selective in his use of ornaments. Not only style, she thought, but an eye for proportion and colour — an artistic flair that showed in every room, every hallway.

And while some of the furniture was simply elegant — even rather grand — there was comfort everywhere.

Chairs were meant to be sat on and sofas to be lounged in, and in the library, huge leather armchairs for curling up with a book. And carpets and rugs that set off each room to perfection. He had made it a home.

His office made a total contrast. Functional to the last detail, it spoke of careful planning and an enthusiasm for high-tech equipment. Filing cabinets, wall maps, and a huge L-shaped desk that dominated the room. A fax machine, two computers, two monitors and two printers made her smile.

'You're ambidextrous?'

He gave her a lop-sided grin. 'You just never know. If I'm to have the luxury of living here, then I need to be equipped for any eventuality, like a computer going down.'

'You'll have a secretary?' she asked casually.

'Not here. There's staff in Adelaide and Melbourne, but here I like to run things alone. I've got office managers to sort out hiring and firing and hassles like that.' For some reason, the answer pleased her.

Some rooms were still bare, notably the bedrooms. 'I'm still sleeping next to the kitchen,' he said. 'I've not yet found what I want for the upper level.' He suddenly turned towards her. 'Now where are you going to sleep tonight?'

'Oh, anywhere will do,' she answered hurriedly. 'One of those deep sofas downstairs and a blanket or two will be fine.'

'Or you could have my bed and I'll — '

'No,' she interrupted even more hurriedly. 'No, one of the sofas will be fine.'

He grinned at her and said nothing.

The microwave pinged as they reached the kitchen and Connor set to work with a can opener. 'I want to grow some vegetables when I get straight — at least, I'll have to hire a gardener. I mustn't get carried away and forget that all this — ' he waved an arm in the direction of the rest of the house,

' — won't be possible if the business isn't flourishing. And for it to continue to flourish, I need to put in long hours and a fair bit of travelling — which will preclude much in the way of fruit and vegetable production — on my part, anyway.'

He pulled out a Barossa Valley riesling from the refrigerator and made a comical presentation of the label for her approval, the bottle draped with a tea towel. Entering into the humour, she nodded solemnly and then delicately tasted the small amount he'd poured.

'That will be fine,' she said graciously.

'Which is just as well, madam, since it's the only chilled one I have.'

A tin of new potatoes, another of baby carrots and some frozen peas, the microwave working overtime to get them piping hot, and then they sat down to a meal that, under the circumstances, even a chef would be pleased with.

'Talking of flourishing businesses,

Natalie, how is yours going?' Connor asked, after a few mouthfuls.

'Very well, finally. It was a bit slow taking off, but after we'd had a few successes, the word got around and people realized that even if one of us was a woman, we knew what we were doing.' She kept her eyes firmly on the food.

He chuckled. 'Touche!' He took a sip of wine. 'You certainly knew what you were doing out there today,' and he jerked his head towards the back of the house. 'You should have a medal for that.'

She looked into her glass and smiled. 'It was a bit hairy at times, Connor. I had visions of the entire contents of the pool suddenly bursting through and submerging me.'

Now his face was serious. 'I don't know how I can ever show my gratitude enough, Natalie. And thank heavens no harm came to you. If you had been submerged, I'd never have forgiven myself.'

She laughed. 'I can swim like a fish, Connor.' She scooped up the last of her chicken. 'In any case, it wouldn't have been your fault. It's the previous owners who need their heads examined for allowing a pool to be built where it was.'

He poured boiling water into the Bodum to filter through and then he opened a can of peaches. She watched him moving competently around the kitchen and reflected that there was nothing effeminate in the fact that he was organizing a meal with skill and relaxed confidence. After all, she reflected, most chefs are men.

'You're quite self-reliant, aren't you, Connor? You give me the impression that you are used to looking after yourself.' She spoke casually. OK, so she was fishing for information — where's the harm in that?

'I've had to, for quite a while now.' His face gave nothing away. 'In any case, I enjoy preparing a meal and cooking it. Not that this one was exactly *haute cuisine*!' He slapped a dollop of ice-cream on each serving. 'Just keep your fingers crossed that the electricity doesn't get cut off for any reason. I'm an ice-creamaholic — I've got enough in there for six months.'

On cue, the lights went off.

She sat in the semi-darkness, her spoon in midair. He uttered a strong Australian expletive that put her in mind of Hamish and then pushed the ice-cream container back into the freezer. After a moment or two glaring at the fridge, he spoke.

'I'll take out what we'll need for the next few hours and then not open the doors again. With luck, they'll have it fixed before too long. Just as long as it's widespread and someone lets them know — which we can't do.' Fumbling a bit in the dark fridge, he pulled out Brie and a litre of milk and a punnet of cherry tomatoes.

'There is a torch — somewhere. And, would you believe, I found some candles the other day, when I was showing the cleaning lady around.'

More fumbling in cupboards and then a triumphant 'Got 'em! And there are some matches.'

He struck a match, lit two candles, each in their holders, and placed them on the table. For a moment, he gazed at her. 'Nothing like candlelight to give a romantic feel to a meal — even if it's at the kitchen table.'

She laughed. 'You must have sixth sense. D'you realize, you got the Bodum going just in time? And all that food — enough for a month. Or is it a siege mentality?'

He shrugged. 'Shopping's a bore so I try to do one massive attack on the supermarket and then forget about it for as long as I can. We just hit the jackpot this time — I could have been down to scraps.'

He insisted they carried the coffee into the drawing-room, and she followed with the two candlesticks, the flames flickering as she walked. 'I feel a bit like

Florence Nightingale,' she said with a smile.

'In jeans. Which would have been much more practical in the Crimea than those voluminous skirts.' He paused, the tray still in his hands and looked at her with a soft expression in his eyes. 'I'd like to see you in voluminous skirts and all the rest of it. Not that jeans don't suit you,' he added hastily. 'It's just that I have a weakness for — well — '

'Voluminous skirts,' Natalie said, 'and low-cut bodices and frilled sleeves and ringlets dangling on necks.' She grinned at him and placed the candlesticks on the mantelpiece. 'I do believe you are a romantic! And not just about candlelight.'

'As a matter of fact,' he said slowly, still holding the coffee tray, and watching her as she kicked off her shoes and curled up on one of the sofas, 'I am, hopelessly. Don't you realize, I fixed that power-cut just so we'd be forced to use the candles?'

'Oh, really? Then why the strong language when it happened?'

'That was just to fool you!' Grinning, he set down the coffee on the low table between the two sofas. The exotic colours of the large Chinese rug complemented the honey-coloured upholstery of the sofas, and the polished wooden floors had a patina that reflected the soft flames of the candles.

Then he set a match to the fire already laid in the roomy fireplace. 'She's a good person, Mrs Partridge. I advertised in the local rag and she's ideal for the job. She has her own car, she works like a Trojan and she even does things without being asked, like laying the fire here.' And he cocked his head towards the flames that roared up the chimney.

'I know her, Connor. She's totally reliable. A bit of a gossip, but that shouldn't worry you.' She gave him a sideways look. 'I'm sure you lead a blameless life.'

He chuckled. 'Most of the time,' he answered. Natalie looked up quickly. Now what's that supposed to mean? He poured out the coffee and handed her a cup. Then he wandered over to a low wooden chest. 'If we are to be stuck here for some time, however pleasant the company is, then we must have some music.'

The chest opened up to reveal a stereo. 'I'm a bit old-fashioned,' he remarked. 'I don't want banks of speakers and woofers or tweeters, or whatever they're called, all in metallic black. Ruins the ambience!' He selected a record and placed it carefully on the turntable. 'Just a selection of records and two good speakers.'

He clicked a switch. Nothing happened. 'Ah.' He looked at her ruefully. 'One forgets . . . ' With a grin, he stretched out on the other sofa.

Outside, it had started to rain again but inside, with a fire crackling in the grate, and sipping hot coffee, Natalie felt suddenly overwhelmed with a feeling of happiness.

He is such good company, she thought, looking across to where, with eyes closed, he was leaning back on the sofa. His feet, clad only in socks, rested on the low table.

Her eyes softened. People look so vulnerable with their eyes closed, she thought. He may be the high-powered businessman but there was a boyish curve to his lips that the macho beard failed to hide and his dark hair flopped over his forehead untidily. I could love that man, she realized, with a sudden shock of truth.

His eyes opened as if, somehow, the jolt that her thoughts had given her, had been transmitted to him. For a moment, he watched her thoughtfully from under dark eyelashes as she hastily lifted the cup to her lips. 'And what's going on in that devious mind of yours?' he asked.

'Nothing of any importance,' she lied. A great deal was going on, but it would have to be kept to herself.

Suddenly to realize, almost without warning, that she had reached a point of no return, was alarming. She had known how he was affecting her physically, but that was a normal reaction, she had decided, of a healthy woman to an attractive man.

But to feel a gentler emotion, a loving wish to place a kiss on those lips, a strong temptation to hold him in her arms just as he had held her when she had cried — all those added up to something more than passion. Natalie, that way lies pain, she told herself fiercely, while her face remained impassive. She needed time to adjust her feelings, to understand what it was that was making her tremble.

For trembling she was, and it made him jump up and take another piece of mallee root from the wicker basket. He threw it on the fire, sending sparks flying up the chimney. 'I'm a rotten host — you're cold!' He took one of her hands in his.

At that moment the lights came on

again. He had left the low lamps on when they had returned to the kitchen after the conducted tour. It was a soft-hued light that illuminated the room — not much more power than the candles.

This time, the stereo did its job. Music swirled softly and she looked around the room. The speakers were half-hidden but still effective. 'Come and dance — it'll warm you up.'

Dance? Be held in his arms while she was still coming to terms with the fact that she was — her thoughts framed the words tentatively — in love with him? Oh, no! She nearly panicked but, instead, she gently took her hand out of his and reached again for the coffee cup.

'The coffee will get cold, Connor. How about telling me more of the development plans? It seems I'm a bit out of touch.'

He didn't seem put out by her refusal, returning to his seat and stretching out again. He talked. He told her of the plans for the freezing-plant at the new factory that was being built, of his agent who had contacted the local growers to ensure a supply of seasonal vegetables. He told her about the new units and the ease with which the plans had passed council and the foundations that were already being poured. He told her of a new shopping mall that would be built on the spare ground in She-Oak Road and of how he had raised finance from interested investors in Adelaide.

But he made no mention of the hall and she didn't ask. It would be too contentious, she knew. And at this moment, with music in the background and a warm feeling — however alarming it might be — of this new-found knowledge of her love for him, she didn't want to break the spell with any more criticisms.

After nearly an hour, he stopped. The music had died and he got up to put on another record. 'More of the same, I think,' and before she could object, he pulled her up to dance. 'This time you can't find an excuse, Natalie,' he said softly, as he urged her towards the smooth, polished floor at the edge of the rug.

It was soft, heart-breakingly sentimental music. In the big room, with almost no light coming from the windows and the soft glow from the table lamps leaving great pools of shadows in the far corners, they danced slowly, his arms holding her close to him, while she struggled to maintain her composure.

The warmth of his body, pressed against hers, was impossible to ignore. He felt strong and fit and his arm around her back sent shivers of awareness over her skin. There was the tangy smell of his soap tickling her nostrils and there was an indefinable scent of maleness that complemented the warmth of his body.

She closed her eyes. I am lost, she thought. I don't know if he's married, I don't know if he's committed in any other way, I don't even know if he thinks of me as a special person but, whatever — I'm lost. OK, so he kissed me once, and he makes all sorts of wicked innuendoes, but isn't that what he'd do in the same circumstances with others?

She tried to disassociate herself from the thoughts that tumbled through her brain. Think of something else, she told herself. Don't think of the way in which his closeness was reducing her insides to water and making it almost impossible for her legs to obey her commands.

'Natalie,' he whispered, his mouth treacherously close to her ear.

'Mm?' she answered, trying to make the single syllable sound casual.

'Natalie, look at me.' He had pulled her right hand close to his chest and his other arm held her even more closely.

Her eyes opened to meet his. And then he bent his head slowly, to take her lips in a kiss that she couldn't avoid. A soft prickling of his beard only served to highlight the tender feel of his mouth on hers.

She returned his kiss willingly, all pretence gone. And, clinging to him in the half-light of the warm room, she thought hazily: I'll pay for this, I know. But for these few moments, it will be worth it.

7

She closed her eyes again. She wanted to savour the feel of him, the musky smell of him and she could do this better with her eyes closed.

It wasn't a demanding kiss. It didn't alarm her. It was tender and loving but it still had a devastating effect on her emotions. Her hand crept up his neck, feeling the bristly hair on his nape and then burying itself in the soft thick growth. He gave a little sigh of pleasure as he felt her fingers in his hair.

After a moment he drew back and her eyes flew open. His expression was enigmatic.

She wasn't sure how long they danced, moving together as one, while the music drifted from one haunting tune to another. After the kiss, he still held her close, his beard, virile and a little prickly, just touching her cheek.

When the record finished, he stood holding her for a moment, as if reluctant to let go. Then he sighed. 'That was — '

' — dreamy,' she finished, with a little laugh and pulled gently away from him. No matter how much the real world invaded their lives, no matter what possibly uncomfortable truths would be revealed about him, she would have had a time of sheer joy in his arms.

She avoided his eyes as she gathered up the coffee cups and placed them on the tray. Picking it up, she moved towards the kitchen. 'There's a stack of washing-up out there,' she murmured prosaically.

'Are you always so — practical?'

'Most of the time, yes. It's my nature.' But there were other aspects of her nature, and they were clamouring to be heard. Aspects that she had thought were buried along with her feelings for Gary. Aspects that threatened to topple her organized life, her plans for the future, her goals. And as she heard him padding along the corridor behind her, she wondered how she would cope with the disillusionment that was bound to follow.

★ ★ ★

'It's fine, Connor, just fine,' she insisted, arranging blankets on the sofa. He looked worried.

'Now the cool change has come in, it'll be chilly tonight, Natalie. I wish you'd take my doona.'

The doona was the last thing she wanted. A potent reminder of Gary — almost an emblem — the sight of it would bring all kinds of unpleasant connotations. So? It should serve to keep in front of her mind that this new relationship, hurtling along in a way she could never have anticipated, could bring as much pain as the former one. Therefore, her logical mind said, take it! Take the doona and keep looking at it and then you won't do anything silly — like falling in love.

Too late, her heart said. Much, much too late.

'Truly, I prefer blankets — more adaptable to changes in the temperature.' Which was a load of nonsense — doonas could be shaken all ways to get them just right.

They had washed up the dishes together, somehow managing to move from the emotion-charged atmosphere of the dancing to the practical tasks in the kitchen. It had actually been fun. Connor had seemed high-spirited and his jokes had sparked off her innate sense of the ridiculous.

Then he had apologized and reluctantly spent some time in the office. No phone yet, which meant no fax. But Natalie had heard the printer grinding away once or twice as she'd surveyed the books in the library.

'Help yourself to any of them, Natalie. Most of them were left behind but there are some of mine, too.'

It was a wide-ranging collection and she'd spent an hour dipping into local history, finding the book he had referred to earlier that recorded the background of Seymour Rise from its earliest days to the postwar era. She'd picked up some of his school prizes: 'Awarded to Connor Sebastian Grant for excellence in Mathematics and Science.' It seemed he had got a prize for those subjects each year. 'Sebastian'? She'd giggled. She'd bring that out on the right occasion, she'd decided.

In the end she'd collected an armful and transferred them to the firelit drawing-room just as she heard him come out of the office.

They'd eaten the Brie with crispbread and tomatoes and he'd had the foresight to chill a bottle of Barossa champagne. 'Shouldn't really call it champagne,' he'd remarked. 'The French get a bit uptight. But I can't get out of the habit. The word has a ring of luxury and bubbly good-humour.'

It was one of the better champagnes and they'd both solemnly agreed that there was nothing quite like it, ' — to seal a friendship,' he'd added. He'd raised his glass to her and then sipped, watching her over the rim until she'd found herself blushing.

And now she was sifting through the books by the sofa and was getting ready to settle down. Except that she didn't feel like settling down at all. The champagne still bubbled, both in the glass and inside her psyche.

Connor walked over to the stereo and put on another record. 'OK, if you refuse to take the doona, then I think we should have a last dance to make sure you're warm when you get under the covers.' There was a smouldering look in his eyes and she should have been warned.

It was a colourful tango that insinuated itself into the room, a sensual beat that made her want to sway to its message. And he wasted no time in wrapping his arms around her and moving in time to the rhythm. It was heady stuff, made more so by the effects of the champagne.

After a minute of whirling her around, with a grin on his face to show his enjoyment, Connor suddenly reacted to a change in the tone of the music. It had become quieter, a more insistent note emphasizing its sensual message. He stopped and put his hand at the nape of her neck and winding his fingers into her hair, pulled back her head.

This was a different kiss, a demanding kiss, a kiss that sent alarm bells ringing. And his other hand stroked her neck and then pulled gently at her boat-shaped neckline. His intentions were clear and she panicked.

'No! No, Connor!' She pulled away from him and stood, her breasts heaving with emotion. 'No, I — we're — it's not what I want!'

His eyes were wild for a moment, as he stood, legs apart and breathing heavily, his beard seeming to quiver with frustration. His voice was harsh: 'I don't think you know what you want. Your body is sending me strong messages, but then your — twitchiness — is taking over.' He stared into her eyes. 'Natalie, something has happened to you which has spoilt your life, I'm sure of that. You're afraid to let your real nature show.'

She started to turn away, her lips trembling, but he shot out a hand and grabbed her wrist in an iron grip. 'Listen to me! You can't go on refusing to let your emotions point the way for you. You can't go on acting like a repressed spinster aunt all your life. There have been several occasions when I glimpsed a passionate, sensual woman — until the shutters came down with a thump.'

She struggled to free her wrist — she didn't want to listen to him. It was too close to the bone. He had discovered the truth without much effort at all, and it unnerved her. But he refused to let go.

'I haven't finished, so you can stop trying to get away. Listen, Natalie Jensen, you once challenged me with a look and I took up that challenge. And I'm going to show you that there is something between you and me that is going to come to a passionate conclusion.'

Suddenly he let go of her wrist — so suddenly that she staggered and sat down abruptly on the sofa.

'But I can wait for it. I can wait until the truth of what I'm saying hits you. Then I won't need to be persuading you — that's not my way. You'll come to me with open arms. And I'll be waiting to satisfy you.'

He turned abruptly and strode out of the room closing the door rather too noisily behind him.

* * *

'You can't go on refusing to let your emotions point the way for you . . . ' Emotions! Did he really think she was going to organize her life according to her emotions? They were unreliable, they landed you in trouble and they brought so much pain that there was no way she would let them 'point the way'.

She sat up in the darkness and rearranged the cushions and the blankets. It must be at least three o'clock and she still hadn't slept. Damn Connor Grant! He was probably sleeping peacefully, totally unaware of the turmoil he had aroused in her by his harsh words.

Natalie stood up and wandered to the window. Outside, in the branches of a eucalyptus, she could hear a mopoke owl hooting mournfully at precisely regular intervals — they must have an inherent sense of rhythm, she reflected. *And I feel as mournful as they sound.*

She quietly opened the window and took a deep breath of the scent of rain-washed earth. In the faint light, she could see the terraces, already looking neater. From a neighbouring property, she heard the gentle lowing of cattle.

I love this place, she thought. *It has*

a peace about it that heals the soul — and I need something like that. Tonight has changed things for ever and I'm not sure I feel able to cope with its significance.

She closed the window and sat on the sofa again. If I could only get a glass of hot milk . . . But the kitchen was next to his room — too dangerous.

Half-an-hour later she decided to live dangerously and get the milk. She pulled on socks — her desert boots were still drying out. Connor had threatened to put them in the microwave for thirty seconds on 'Low' but she had laughingly taken them out of his hands and said it was too risky. 'There's nothing in the instruction book about desert boots, whether medium-rare or well-done.'

Taking one of the candles from the mantelpiece, she lit it and moved softly and carefully along the corridor to the kitchen.

She saw, with relief, that his door was closed. A carton of milk, an

166

earthenware mug and a careful setting of one-and-a-half minutes on the microwave. She clicked open the door just as the 'ping' sounded and held her breath for a moment.

'While you're at it, you could heat some for me.'

She whirled around, nearly dropping the mug. He stood wide-eyed in the doorway, a towel tucked around his waist. 'Finding it hard to sleep — must be the thunder in the air.' There is no thunder in the air, she wanted to say, so that's not the reason. When she had leant out of the window earlier, the air had been fresh and the sky clear. But a comment like that would only lead to trouble.

The sight of his half-naked body brought the realization of their intimate situation. Only a T-shirt and bikini pants — her usual nightwear — covered her. She turned away quickly to hide her confusion.

He strolled to the table, not the slightest bit embarrassed, it seemed, and sat down. Neither of them spoke as his mug of milk was heated. She handed it to him and sat at the opposite side of the table. The silence continued as each of them sipped at the soothing warmth.

Then he put his mug down. 'Natalie,' he started tentatively. She looked up. 'Natalie, I'm sorry if I sounded off earlier. I guess I shouldn't have let my feelings run away with me.'

She shrugged. 'It was just the effect of the champagne, Connor. Don't give it another thought. I certainly won't.' Liar, she thought. You've been thinking about it for the past four hours and tomorrow you'll be thinking about it again. But just now, she thought, I don't want any more uncovering of feelings, yours or mine. There are too many potentially explosive factors in any conversation about our relationship and three-fifteen in the morning is not the time to stir it all up again.

She stood up and yawned into her hand. 'Don't give it another thought,' she repeated and walked resolutely out of the kitchen, wishing that she could have made a more dignified exit. The T-shirt was short and didn't quite cover the pants.

★ ★ ★

'It's a beautiful morning, the phone's working again and a bulldozer is on its way.' Connor handed her a steaming cup of tea as she opened her eyes.

He was fully dressed and his hair, still damp from a shower, curled slightly around his ears. A shiver of pleasure ran through Natalie at the sight of him.

'I'm going down to have a look at the chopper. I'm sorry, but the main bathrooms upstairs are not yet finished. So you'll have to use mine. It's off my room and there are clean towels.' He sounded cheerful and practical, as if last night had never happened. 'I'll be back to get some breakfast in about half-an-hour.'

He was making it easy for her, she

realized. Giving her a clear field and even stating the time of his return. She smiled inwardly.

The shower was heaven. She had walked briskly through his room, glancing briefly around her. It was remarkably tidy — for a man, she thought — and the doona was in place. And now the water was hot and she felt a rising of the spirits — except that there was some niggling thought at the back of her mind that she couldn't pin down.

Then she got it. 'The bulldozer is on its way,' he had said. And with the bulldozer moving the tree trunk and pulling her car to safety, it meant that she could drive away, providing the creek was down.

She paused, the towel in her hand stilled. She could drive away. Why did that make her feel desolate? Wouldn't she have driven away before, if she could have?

The operative word was 'before'. Before she had spent nearly twenty-four hours with him. Before he had taken her in his arms. Before he had kissed her. And before she had fallen in love.

She took a sobbing breath and blinked away tears. The enchanted time, with its breathless moments and its joyful moments and with its alarms and its sudden realization of destiny, was over.

★ ★ ★

'Is Mr Grant there?' Mrs Partridge sounded puzzled. The phone had rung before he'd come back from the helicopter and Natalie, after a moment's hesitation, had picked it up and announced the number.

'No, Mrs Partridge,' said Natalie, recognizing the woman's broad Somerset accent. She'd been in Australia for thirty years but there was no mistaking her speech patterns. 'He's out in the paddock but I expect he'll be back before long. Can I take a message?'

'Why, that's Natalie Jensen, isn't

it?' Natalie cursed herself for being so naive. But then she realized there was a way out of a gossip-inducing situation.

'Yes,' she said smoothly, 'I'm working on the garden.' She nearly added, for good measure, something about hearing the phone from outside and coming in to answer it, but decided that it would sound too contrived.

'Oh, yes, of course you are! And I bet you're doing a good job, Natalie. My brother was pleased with the way you landscaped his place.' There was a slight pause. 'But how did you get there? Bob's just been called out to work on the bulldozer gang — I thought he said there was a gum down — from yesterday's storm — over Mr Grant's driveway.'

Damn, thought Natalie. 'Oh, it's a bit of a mess here after the storm, Mrs Partridge, but I was determined to get in and — well, here I am.' No lies, just juggling with words a bit.

There was another pause. Then: 'Yes,

172

well, could you tell Mr Grant that I'd like to come tomorrow? That is, Monday instead of Tuesday, if it's all right with him? I've got a key but I hope he's around anyway. I set that burglar alarm thing off last week. The police were all over the place — not too pleased when they found out it was me.'

'Of course. I'll tell him, Mrs Partridge. If it's not convenient, I expect he'll ring you.'

Natalie put down the phone with a rueful twist to her lips. The woman was an energetic worker but she had this longstanding reputation for putting two and two together and making a scandal. She shrugged. Too late for regrets. Perhaps Bob Partridge wouldn't be too specific when he got home.

★ ★ ★

'There, Natalie, you're free again!' Connor was laughing as he watched the huge, lumbering bulldozer pull the

Suzuki back from the edge of the creek. It hadn't been thought wise for anyone to get in to release the handbrake but, in the event, the wheels slid over the mud without any snags.

Free again? Physically, yes, she thought, looking up sideways into his amused eyes. Emotionally, no. She felt she would always be held by a silken thread to this man standing next to her, his gumbooted legs astride as he put one arm around her waist and gave her a quick hug. She hoped Bob Partridge hadn't seen.

The bulldozer had rumbled up the driveway and over the culvert. Connor had held his breath, not sure about the strength of the concrete bridge. It had crumbling edges but it had supported the front-end loader. 'Bulldozers are heavier still, but I got an engineer out to look at it — among other things — before I let the removal vans get moving. He said it could do with renovating but it was structurally sound.'

And so it proved to be. The fallen tree had been pushed and shoved out of the way first and now, with Natalie's car safe, if a bit mud-spattered, the men were getting to work with a chainsaw on the smaller branches. It may have been Sunday, but they had no religious principles about earning a bit of overtime.

Connor got inside the Suzuki and after a few grumbles from the starter motor, it roared into life. Natalie joined him and they drove back. 'Seems fine, but maybe a check at the local garage wouldn't come amiss,' Connor suggested, as she piled her grip and briefcase in the back.

He stood, in the familiar stance of arms akimbo and legs apart, while she did a U-turn on the gravel. As she drew level with him again, she stopped.

'Thanks for — er — everything,' she murmured.

'It was quite a day,' he responded with a grin. Then he became serious.

'I hope — that is — ' His eyes looked troubled.

What was he trying to say, she wondered. That he was sorry there had been moments of disagreement? That he hoped she wasn't going to assume anything about his behaviour? That he hoped she wasn't going to put too great importance on what had happened after the champagne?

He compressed his lips, seemed to change his mind about finishing the sentence, and started again. 'I hope you haven't caught cold after getting so wet yesterday,' he concluded prosaically.

She nearly laughed out loud. With laughter in her eyes, she pushed her pale hair behind her ears and let in the clutch. 'I'll take lots of Vitamin C,' she assured him and drove off giggling at his banal words.

★ ★ ★

'So there it is, Hamish. The place is in a dreadful mess — mud everywhere — but

176

it solves the problem over what to do with all that water.'

Hamish had laughed himself silly when she'd related the story to him. She'd glossed over the details, but she'd been aware of his eyes watching her face as she told him of Connor's reaction to finding a metre-deep ditch along the back of the house. 'I hope he was grateful for everything you did,' he finally said, still watching her carefully.

'Oh, yes!' she said airily, standing up and moving towards his kitchen door. She didn't want Hamish to ask any more questions.

In any case, she needed to catch up with some jobs around the place and she must go and check on her mother. Mary Jensen was not the happiest person in a thunderstorm. 'It's not that I'm frightened, you understand,' she would say, cringing as the noise crashed around her. 'It's just that I'm — well — a little nervous.' All the difference in the world, Natalie would think, giving her an understanding hug.

Now Hamish walked out to the Suzuki with Natalie, and circled the vehicle, looking for damage. And as she pulled her luggage out, a fast-moving car roared down the road towards them, slowed almost imperceptibly and then gathered speed as it continued to Ashley.

Hamish hadn't noticed. But Natalie watched the back of the dark blue sports car until it rounded the corner and was out of sight.

★ ★ ★

'He wants the upper-floor rooms finished by the end of the week,' she heard the painter say, as he and his colleague sorted out the cans of paint in the toolshed.

'Cripes, that's going it a bit, isn't it? Today's Tuesday.'

'I'll have to see if we can pull in some blokes from the Gawler job.'

Natalie was measuring, with a

surveyor's tape, the pathway at the back of the house. It was hopelessly narrow and, widened, it would make better access to the vegetable garden. Hamish had worked all day on the Monday clearing the mess, filling in the ditch and shaking his head in mock-horror at the mud and the erosion in the rose garden. She'd seen a grin on his face — he had a small boy's delight at scenes of devastation. 'What a mess,' he'd said, but she had a conviction that he'd loved to have been the one sloshing it all around at the height of the storm.

Now the workmen were clattering the paint tins, ready to move into the house. 'What's the panic, then? 'e said there'd be another fortnight before Mrs Grant came.'

Natalie froze. Their voices were clear — there was no mistaking what they were saying.

'Well, apparently the lady's getting impatient. Fed up with Melbourne weather, he said. So she's arriving next weekend and the main bedroom's gotta be ready. Oh, and the big bathroom.'

'The weather 'ere's not been too flash, what's 'er hurry?'

'Doan ask me. You know what women are — never satisfied. She probably wants to keep an eye on him. My guess is he's a bit of a rager — have you seen the way he looks at that gardener woman?'

Natalie could hear them chuckling as she ran, stumbling, down the side of the house to the haven of the Suzuki.

8

Natalie wasn't sure for how long she'd been driving or how she'd got to the top of Mount Memory. She'd simply flung the car out of the driveway and taken the opposite direction to Ashley. Hurling the vehicle around corners, not noticing signposts, just getting as far away as she could from Seymour Rise.

The bitumen had turned into dirt tracks and the dirt tracks had become narrower and had started to climb steeply and still she had punished the accelerator pedal. Then she had come out at the peak of the hill and realized where she was.

And now she turned off the engine and tried to stop her heart thumping. There was a fresh breeze blowing up here and she could see the countryside for kilometres around. She climbed down, thrust the keys into her pocket, and started to trudge along the bush path.

You should have known, she told herself. No one as good-looking as that, with that sort of charm and with that sort of money, could remain single at the age of — whatever. Twenty-five? No, older. Thirty?

'Oh, what the hell does it matter how old he is?' she cried, as tears pricked the back of her eyes. The bush was silent around her. There was no one here to witness her humiliation.

For humiliated she was. She'd fallen for the oldest trick in the book — soft and gentle spaniel-brown eyes allied with a vital, high-powered body; tender and caring manner backed up with an assertive, leave-it-to-me style. And looks that zinged, she thought agonizedly, closing her eyes and seeing his laughter-filled face, with strong white teeth and that black beard bristling with vitality.

She'd reached another clearing and,

unwillingly, her eyes were drawn to the sight of Seymour Rise, a long way away but clearly seen in the limpid air. Its dark windows showed no signs of life at this distance, but there was activity of some sort on the gravel park in front. Cars moving around and tiny figures, but none she could identify.

She wished she'd never seen the place. If only she'd been more brusque at the beginning, he'd probably have employed an Adelaide landscaping firm. It would have cost him a great deal more, with the distance involved, but that wouldn't have worried him. She'd got the impression that he'd been ploughing money back into the business *and* expanding while at the same time carefully saving, and selling his Melbourne home, for a project such as this.

Natalie turned away from the heart-wrenching sight of Seymour Rise and stumbled back to the Suzuki. She climbed inside and sat for some moments, surveying the future. How could she cope with seeing him each day? There was no way she could avoid him.

A sob escaped from her lips and it acted as a watershed for her anguish. Tears poured down her cheeks unchecked, as she recalled those moments of near-surrender when they'd danced. How he must have laughed to himself! And how dare he act as if he were hurt and rejected? He had been filling in the time, so to speak, until his wife arrived. She had been a challenge, just as he had said, a challenge to be taken up so that he could prove himself a man-of-the-world, a conqueror. And if she had been a naive, easily-impressed young girl, he'd have conquered her.

A shiver ran through her at the realization of how close that had been. It was the Gary situation all over again — only three times worse. Gary had never inspired the deep sense of tenderness and devotion she had felt for Connor. It had lain, albeit for a short time, strong and enduring behind the physical attraction.

Enduring? She snorted through her tears. Without a reciprocal devotion on his part, the enduring nature of what she now felt was a mockery of love.

Slowly she straightened her shoulders. Then she reached for the box of tissues in the glove box. And five minutes later, with a stern mouth and empty eyes, she turned the ignition key.

★ ★ ★

'Yes, reinstate the rose garden,' Connor said flatly. 'If it needs fresh loam, then get it.' And he turned on his heel and walked back into the house.

Her heart had slammed into her ribs when he'd appeared an hour ago. She'd arrived back from Mount Memory determined to work like a slave to get the job at Seymour Rise out of the way. It had lost its magic for her. Every time she came here, she'd risk seeing Connor — and that was the last thing she wanted. Natalie watched him going with a frown. OK, so she had been cool and offhand with him but she hadn't expected a matching chilliness in his manner. She'd expected him to be cheerful and confident — just as he had been two days ago, when he'd waved her off the premises.

She swallowed, to move the peculiar lump in her throat. She turned away to where Hamish was waiting. They had put off the decisions about saplings in the main vista until she'd had a chance to get to Adelaide and see Kurt. She'd go next weekend, and with any luck, this time she'd get there — and get some shopping done.

The surveyor and his assistant had pegged out the site for the new pool at the lower level. Now she and Hamish were to plan the layout for the rose garden and see which bushes, if any, could be salvaged.

She hadn't seen Connor at all on the Monday after that fateful weekend, but she'd assumed he'd been working in the office. His car had been under the portico. The workmen all entered the house by the kitchen door now, and used the narrow back staircase, so as not to damage or make dusty the beautiful hall.

But she'd been surprised that he hadn't come out to see her at all. The Suzuki had been parked next to Mrs Partridge's battered old Holden. She had wanted to see him — she had ached to see him. Although the weekend had ended on an indecisive note, he'd been friendly and there'd been that hug when her car had been pulled to safety. Yet she'd neither seen nor heard him the whole day.

Then this morning she'd barely arrived when she'd overheard the nightmarish conversation between the two painters and had made her frantic flight.

Now she decided that, once she had the measurements, she would return to the office and spend some time with gardening catalogues and draw a detailed plan. The excavating for the pool would be too far away to affect the rose garden, so they could set to work right away — the ground would be irrigated by the hillside spring. Rose bushes take time to get established so the work and the ordering of new bushes should take place soon. Maybe this time next year, it would be as he wanted it.

This time next year . . . What would she be doing then? Ashley had suddenly become a desolate place for her — perhaps she would move away. Conflicting emotions about Connor jostled for attention in her mind as she made notes while Hamish called out the dimensions of the plot.

There were other measurements to be made and it was three hours before Natalie climbed, tired and dispirited, into the Suzuki on the gravel. She sat for a moment, planning the next few days. There was so much to do, and she felt like doing nothing. She felt an unaccustomed lethargy that threatened to . . .

She was being watched. She kept her eyes firmly ahead, looking through the windscreen to where the driveway curved away towards the road, and the skin on the back of her neck crawled. She was afraid to look towards the house, but somewhere, at one of those windows, eyes were fixed on her.

Slowly she turned her head. At one of the drawing-room windows Connor stood, hands in the pockets of his moleskins. His face was expressionless, his dark eyes watching her with a hard scrutiny that made her stomach contract.

For a short time, they stared at each other with unsmiling faces. Then she turned the ignition key and moved away as fast as she dared on the unstable gravel surface.

She found her hands trembling on the steering wheel. Pull yourself together, Natalie. Just take one day at a time. Get the work done. You should be glad that his ardour, or whatever it was, appears to have cooled — probably because the reality of his wife's arrival has made him see that there could be no future in his pursuing her. And pursuing her he had been. And you, Natalie Jensen, said the tiny voice, were not exactly breaking the sound barrier to get away from him, right?

Her lip curled in an expression of self-disgust. She'd been an easy prey and he must have — Stop it, she told herself, as she swung the vehicle into the road to Ashley. That way lies so much self-recrimination that you'll be back to the emotional mess you were in not so many years ago.

★ ★ ★

The big Adelaide stores were cosmic, she decided. Ashley wasn't without dress shops but they weren't geared for her age group. They sold teenage stuff and they sold sensible dresses for the local matrons. But for those in between, there was a dearth of stylish outfits with that little bit extra.

Now the business was going well, she deserved some reward for all the twelve-hour days and six-day weeks. The most difficult part was which of the many outfits she glimpsed in the big stores she should buy with the limited amount she'd allowed herself. They were all so right, the colour and textures of the material seducing her into whipping out her credit cards too frequently. Maybe if she could get back into the habit of carrying cash, she'd get a more realistic feeling of spending money, rather than merely signing little pieces of paper.

And just as she was walking back to the car park, with three large plastic bags and the happy knowledge that she could change out of the eternal jeans-and-top every now and then, she saw it.

In the window of a boutique tucked away in a side street, with a discreet 'Sale' sign, the dress, in dark green velvet, with a low-cut square neck and elbow-length sleeves with generous frills, lay draped on the off-white carpet.

She caught her breath in a gasp. It was beautiful and romantic and it spoke of luxury. Plain, with no ornament or embroidery to distract the eye from the deep plushy richness of the material, it beckoned with a siren's insistence.

'No,' she said firmly. 'I've spent enough as it is,' she added, walking on.

'Yes,' she whispered and did a smart U-turn.

'It's the only one we have.' The sales assistant was plump and motherly. 'Actually it was made-to-measure for a customer who changed her mind. The manageress wasn't too happy. But she decided to keep the deposit the customer had paid and offer it in the sale. So it's very reasonable for the quality.' She looked at Natalie's slim figure. 'It might well be your size — would you like to try it on?'

A token moment of hesitation on

Natalie's part and then she was being zipped in. 'Perfect!' came the envious voice of the sales assistant and Natalie turned around to look in the mirror.

For a moment she stared. It wasn't that she was totally without vanity, but looking in the mirror had been an occupation she'd not indulged in for some time. As long as her face was clean and her hair tidy, she'd not bothered to view identical pairs of jeans and cotton T-shirts.

The dark green brought out the colour of her eyes — 'stormy seas' he'd said — and the lush material against her skin gave it a luminous glow. Her corn-coloured hair swung over bare shoulders and her waist looked tiny above the folds of the skirt that reached the ground. She felt a little breathless.

'Oh, that does suit you,' murmured the assistant, looking over her shoulder.

Sanity returned. 'How much?' Natalie asked and nearly fell over at the answer.

'But it's a classic, dear. With that in your wardrobe and different jewellery — or a scarf — you could wear it year in and year out.'

'I'd need to wear it for breakfast, lunch and dinner to get full value.' She swayed from one foot to another and the material whispered softly around her legs.

'Come out and look at it in the salon. You can get a better idea than in this little fitting-room.'

It was even more breathtaking in the long view and Natalie knew she had to have it. Seeing that I've never had an evening dress in my life and seeing that there's the local hunt ball in August and that I've been invited by someone-or-other, I have to have it.

It wasn't until she was walking out of the boutique with the heavy dress swathed in tissue-paper and reverently packed in a large box, that Natalie realized that it had a 'voluminous skirt' and a 'low-cut bodice' and 'frilled sleeves'. Her words of a week ago came whispering into her mind. Ringlets dangling on her neck? It could be done without too much trouble, by the local hairdresser, she thought.

She stood stock-still on the pavement, her arms loaded with parcels. Whatever was she thinking of? A sudden vision of Connor rose in front of her as he was that night, holding the tray of coffee cups and looking at her with undisguised admiration — and more? — as she turned towards him with the candles.

Her eyes filled with hot tears and she moved to one side as another woman shopper snapped 'Excuse me' and brushed past her.

★ ★ ★

Kurt was a godsend. He looked at the photos and narrowed his eyes and asked a lot of questions and then set to work with pencil and paper. In two hours he had sorted out the problem and they were reminiscing over a pot of tea.

He had been delighted to see her and after the tea they walked in his garden while he pointed out new hybrids and showed her his collection of roses. He was limping a bit, she noticed and his hair seemed greyer than ever.

'Time's catching up with me, Natalie. I've had disconcerting news from the specialist about my leg, so my gardening days are numbered.' His hand on her shoulder gripped a little tighter. 'Enjoy life while you can, child. Gather ye rosebuds and all that — you never know what nasty tricks fate has up its sleeve.'

Planting rose bushes was the nearest she'd get to gathering rosebuds, she thought grimly. To have been fooled twice in four years didn't say much for her judgment. She toyed with the idea of telling Kurt about it, but then decided against it. He was a wise old fellow, but problems of the heart — her heart — had to be solved in isolation.

'You're looking a bit peaky, Natalie. Anything wrong?'

'No, Kurt, nothing,' she lied. 'Been working hard, that's all.'

He gave her a thoughtful look but, thankfully, he left it at that. And as she waved goodbye to him early on Monday, having spent two restless nights in the narrow bed under the eaves of his cottage, she wondered how long it would be before she saw him again and whether he'd still be mobile when she did.

The journey back was uneventful, which was just as well, she thought guiltily, realizing her concentration had not been on the traffic. It had been on the man she had last seen staring at her through a window, his face grim and unsmiling. But she was travelling in the opposite direction to the commuters and, at seven o'clock in the morning the road was almost empty.

She would go straight to Seymour Rise — it would save time. Kurt had given her a breakfast of bacon and eggs with gallons of coffee despite her protests. 'I never eat breakfasts like this, Kurt.'

'Then perhaps it's time you did,' he'd responded calmly. 'You're not looking like the energetic Natalie I remember.'

'I was five years younger then.'

'Oh, sure. And now you're over the hill, I suppose.'

She grinned as she turned into the driveway. It was nice to have him clucking over her like a father.

Her eyes flew to the portico. Connor's car was there. And, at the back of the house, Hamish was waiting for her. 'He's a bit cranky today, Nat. Been out here once and seemed put out you weren't around. I've been here off and on for most of the weekend, but he was away. He wanted to talk to you about the roses.'

'It's only eight o'clock. What time does he expect us to be here?'

Hamish shrugged. 'Wanted to know if you'd ordered them yet. It sounded as if he had some ideas about the types.'

So Mrs Grant had arrived, Natalie surmised. His wife had arrived and she probably wanted a say in the matter. She stiffened as she heard the kitchen door slam. Then footsteps. Two sets of footsteps, and one made clacking noises. High heels, she thought, and took a deep breath as she turned around.

'Mother, I'd like you to meet Natalie Jensen. Natalie, this is my mother, Elizabeth Grant. She arrived yesterday. She's come to keep an eye on me.'

A white-haired figure, dressed in a fine-knit, mushroom-coloured suit, walked towards her, one hand held out. As Natalie struggled to control her sagging jaw, Elizabeth Grant smiled and said: 'I've heard such a lot about you and the work you're doing. And what I've seen so far is a credit to you.'

After she'd shaken Natalie's hand, she turned to Hamish. 'And you must be Hamish MacIntyre. I'm delighted to meet you, too.'

Waves of — what? Of joy? Of relief? Of laughter? Whatever, Natalie felt a surge of emotion that threatened to make her hysterical. She looked at Connor and had to fight with an almost uncontrollable urge to run and put her arms around him.

Except that his face was impassive. His eyes were the hard gemstones she had seen once before and his arms were folded across his chest. His body language was sending her messages to 'keep off'.

Elizabeth Grant was twinkling up at Hamish now, and Hamish was loving it. Natalie looked again at Connor, puzzled at the stern, unyielding expression on his face.

'My mother's got some ideas about roses. If you've got some spare time, you could get together.' He spoke without animation. 'And now I must get on.' He turned to his mother and his expression softened. 'Going to Adelaide, Mother. I won't be back until tomorrow evening. You won't mind being alone?'

'Connor,' Elizabeth answered with a laugh, 'when have I ever minded being alone?'

He turned abruptly, giving Natalie and Hamish a curt nod, and disappeared into the house.

'Natalie, if you have time now, I'll get some more suitable shoes on, and we could look at what's survived the — er — flood.' She was smiling and it was obvious she knew about the previous weekend's drama. Her eyes were unnervingly like Connor's, but a soft brown where his had been stony. But as Natalie agreed with the suggestion, she remembered a time when he'd looked at her with that same gentle gaze.

Half-an-hour later, her feet now clad in sensible brogues, Elizabeth sat drinking coffee with Natalie as they perched on a low wall by the rose garden. While they'd been checking on the bushes, the sports car had pulled away from the front of the house with Connor at the wheel. He'd waved at the two of them, but only Elizabeth responded. Natalie made a quick decision that, in his present mood, a light and cheery wave from her would not be welcome.

'There are quite a few roses I like out there, Natalie. And if you're happy with the others I've chosen, it should be a wonderful sight next year.'

Connor's mother was knowledgeable about horticulture. She'd had a small garden back in Melbourne, she'd said, but the climate was so different here in South Australia. 'I'm looking forward to pottering around here, except that . . . ' Her voice tailed away and she looked around her at the expanse of garden and the vista to Mount Memory.

'It's so big, Natalie. I feel a little overwhelmed. Oh, it's going to be beautiful when it's all landscaped,' she added hastily, as if she might have offended Natalie. 'But there's to be at least one full-time gardener, for the vegetable garden and the terraces, and — well — it won't seem like a personal garden. I like to sow seeds and plant seedlings and have pots and things . . . ' Her voice tailed away again.

Natalie looked at her thoughtfully. She understood perfectly. Obviously Connor hadn't anticipated this. This woman needed her own little plot, where she could decide what and where and when. Not just a corner of someone else's.

Suddenly it came to her. 'A courtyard, that's what you need! With paving and walls and some small flower beds and some planters for herbs and — '

Elizabeth's eyes were shining. 'Oh yes, Natalie, that would be marvellous! Is it possible? But where?'

'Let's walk around a bit,' responded Natalie. And they trudged around the house, with Natalie's imagination working overtime. If there were a built-in alcove somewhere, it could be extended without too much expense. There was a pile of weathered old bricks behind one of the stables — she'd noticed them the week before. They'd be ideal for the paving.

At the side of the house, where the dining-room's French windows opened onto a neglected patch of weed-scattered gravel, she uttered a low cry of discovery. 'Perfect! Look, Mrs Grant! You can walk straight out here, there are steps down, there are overhanging eaves and the walls can be extended without much difficulty. What do you think?'

'We could even have meals out here when the weather's right! Oh, and Natalie — please call me Elizabeth.'

Natalie smiled. Already she liked this woman and she felt confident a courtyard would make all the difference to her happiness in the new life that had been — Natalie hesitated in her thoughts — thrust upon her?

'When can you start on it?' Elizabeth was fired with enthusiasm.

'I can draw up a plan and cost it tonight. Then I — that is, you — could ask Connor.' She felt a bit of a coward, but in the current frosty climate, it would be better that way.

'No need,' said Elizabeth airily, smoothing her white hair with a capable hand. 'I have money of my own. *I* shall pay for it, and Connor need not know anything about it until it's finished.'

Why is it, thought Natalie, that I feel a flutter of anxiety about that?

9

It had been a week since Connor's mother had arrived, and the plans for the courtyard had moved fast. Natalie had drawn up the plans and a rough sketch of what she imagined could be done with planters, low benches, some potted citrus trees and even a tiny fountain. Elizabeth had been enchanted.

As it happened Connor had been away for longer than a day. Then he was back for only thirty-six hours before flying to Melbourne. His land development business was going through some sort of staff crisis, Elizabeth reported vaguely to Natalie. 'Someone was promoted and someone else thought it should have been them. The office politics can get a bit complex at times, but, thankfully, everyone seems to want to stay there. There's a great deal of loyalty towards Connor,' added Elizabeth with a barely-disguised pleased look on her face.

The way in which his mother took Natalie into her confidence was surprising, but Natalie put it down to loneliness on the part of the older woman. She needed a confidante and she seemed to find Natalie a trustworthy recipient of all sorts of snippets of information.

Without probing in the slightest, Natalie had learnt a great deal about the family background. Elizabeth often wandered out to join her, absent-mindedly pulling out a weed as she talked. One day she insisted on Natalie and Hamish joining her for lunch mainly, she said, 'Because I'm rather proud of my asparagus omelet.'

Natalie learned of how Connor had reluctantly given up the idea of veterinary studies because of the cost of study over six years, with little financial assistance in the way of scholarship grants; of how he had worked long hours as an employee of a large firm in Melbourne, while studying part-time for his degree in accountancy; and of how he had borrowed money to set up his own business and had been so successful that the loan was paid back within five years.

Elizabeth was palpably proud of her son. 'He never had time for romance, though, and that's something I feel sad about,' she had said one day as they shared scones and tea on the steps overlooking the shambles that would soon be her courtyard. 'Oh, there have been girlfriends — some of them quite pleasant, too — but somehow he never got committed,' she added, spreading butter on the hot scone.

Perhaps he went all moody on them, Natalie had thought. Perhaps he blew hot and cold and they couldn't stand the suspense. Whatever, she thought gloomily, the distance that had now developed between her and Connor was too great to be overcome, whether he was in Melbourne, Adelaide or the next room. Whatever illusions she might have had about his feelings towards her, whether or not she was prepared to take a chance on having her heart broken again, it was all academic.

Natalie decided to change the subject. Somehow, she couldn't bear to talk about Connor and his girlfriends, pleasant or otherwise. 'Elizabeth, it — um — won't be possible to do everything here without Connor seeing it, you know. The drainage pipes have been laid, and the foundations for the walls will go in tomorrow — it will all be a bit obvious.'

Elizabeth looked thoughtful. 'Leave it to me. I'll think of something. We don't have many meals in the dining-room anyway. One or two dinners a week, if he's here. And this time of the year, with dark evenings, I draw the curtains over those windows, so he won't see a thing. Breakfast we have in the kitchen and other meals in front of the fire in the drawing-room.' She gave Natalie a mischievous look.

There was a lull now in Natalie's work at Seymour Rise. The saplings for the vista to Mount Memory had not yet arrived, the roses had been planted, a day-by-day gardener had been employed by Natalie, acting on a terse note left for her by Connor, and the pool was a hive of activity. Until that was finished, the final touches to the surrounds couldn't be added.

Hamish would lay the paving for the courtyard and he'd subcontracted a bricklayer mate to put up the walls once the foundations were dry. Natalie had put aside other jobs to make sure the courtyard plans moved ahead quickly.

So she drove away one evening knowing that it would be a week before she needed to go out to the big house again. They'd been awarded the commission for the hospital grounds and materials had to be ordered. Tomorrow she would spend a short time checking Mrs. Travers' fountain — it had performed beautifully while her visitors were there, but now it was getting temperamental. Then it would be time to get her nose to the grindstone with the hospital project.

She was particularly pleased about that. The other tenderers had been big city firms and a landscaping firm from Gawler but, for some reason, her tender had been accepted. 'They just liked yours the most, Natalie,' Clive had told her. 'It wasn't the lowest tender — but it wasn't the highest. And, in any case, they preferred to give the contract to a local firm.'

As she slowed before turning in to the driveway of her place, her heart leapt at the sight of Connor's car coming from Ashley. And then it started hammering furiously as she realized he was stopping. She continued, turning the Suzuki across the road in front of his now-stationary vehicle. As she climbed down, he unfolded himself from the sports car and strolled over to where she was locking hers.

'Thought I might have missed you,'

he drawled. He was wearing a beautifully-cut charcoal suit with a white shirt and a red tie. Almost a uniform for businessmen, she thought, but he gives it something more. It's not fair, she thought fleetingly, he looks devastating in whatever he wears, from gumboots and parka to — this. He even looks devastating dressed simply in a towel. And then a flush of red swept over her cheeks at the memory of that night.

He gave her a lazy, knowing look as he glimpsed her blush. It was almost as if he knew what she was thinking. But that's ridiculous, she thought, trying to calm her emotions.

'How long will the work take now?' he asked, looking past her shoulder to the windows of the cottage. Hamish had built the place with the two front doors at each side, so as to maintain the privacy of the occupants. From the front, she suddenly realized, it looked like one residence.

'Hard to say exactly,' she answered,

matching the cool note of his voice. 'Until the pool is complete, and tested, I'm not prepared to finish off the surrounds with the vegetation you want. It'd be better to put it off.' She had no need to mention the courtyard — it was at the opposite end of the house.

He was propping himself against the side of the Suzuki, his legs crossed at the ankle and the defensive pose of arms across his chest that she'd seen before. The body language was loud and clear: I'm keeping myself to myself.

His eyes swept over her, from her mud-encrusted gumboots and torn jeans, over the thick jumper and up to her hair, straggling out of a ponytail and with bits of leaf and grass left from when she'd been fighting with a blackberry bush that had to be grubbed out.

One corner of his mouth lifted in amusement. 'You certainly get into the spirit of the thing, don't you?'

Suddenly, she felt angry. Here he

was, breaking her heart with his aloofness — more than that, his hostility, inexplicable and wounding — and he had the nerve to criticise her appearance.

Her chin came up. 'So you see, I can't answer your question precisely — it will depend on other workers and, to some extent, the weather. And I've been working since seven this morning,' she bit out. 'I'm tired and I'm hungry and I just want to be left in peace to have a shower.' She turned on her heel, but not before she had seen his eyes widen and a reluctant look of admiration come into his face.

As she stalked up the path, she could hear him behind her. God, what was he going to do? Come inside? She couldn't stand that. She couldn't stand the proximity — half-a-cottage is small with two people in it.

'Natalie!' She whirled around. 'I also wanted to invite you to a dinner I'm having in four weeks' time — on the twenty-fifth.' She gazed at him, stupefied. 'Christmas-in-June and a housewarming put together. Turkey and — um — Christmas pudding and — things . . . ' His voice tailed off and she still stared at him.

He looked slightly uncomfortable, she thought. Like a small boy talking about a party but feeling that he might be sounding — like a small boy. And that, of course, wounds your macho image, she thought. And that, her honesty forced her to admit, is unwarranted. He's not macho, he's manly. And I love him.

She turned away, not wanting to reveal any of those feelings.

'There'll be dancing and — '

'And Santa Claus and prezzies?' she enquired sarcastically.

She heard him chuckle, the first time for two weeks that there had been any humour in their contact with each other. 'Oh, I don't think we'll go as far as that.' She turned back, her face composed.

He stood looking past her at the

cottage again. 'I have some friends coming over from Melbourne — they're itching to see what sort of a place it is where I've been spending so much time. I have to be sure the inside will be finished, because some of them will be house-guests. So I thought it would be — ah — nice if the outside were finished, too. If it's possible,' he added.

So he wanted to show off, did he? 'As I said,' she remarked, shrugging, 'it mostly depends on others.' She started to walk towards the house. 'As far as I'm concerned, I believe I've got something else organized for the twenty-fifth. Sorry!' She knew she was sounding ungracious, but she couldn't help it. Her heart was hurting too much for her to sound any other way.

He said nothing, but she heard his footsteps receding and then the sports car door opening and slamming in quick succession.

And as he pulled away, he had to slow momentarily to let Hamish's truck pull in to the driveway and park behind the Suzuki.

* * *

'It is simply lovely, Natalie. I'm delighted. And next week I'm going to take a trip to the plant nursery and get all sorts of things.' Elizabeth was beside herself with excitement. 'Just wait till Connor sees it!'

Yes, thought Natalie, just wait. Somehow, his mother had succeeded in hiding it from him, but today he would see it. And he would see that a great deal of work had gone into it, without his being consulted in any way. OK, so he'd given her more-or-less a free hand with the details of the work on the property, but only after the basic decisions had been made, mainly by him. And though he wasn't paying for the work on the courtyard — not that that would have worried him unduly, she guessed — it had been done without his knowledge and approval and she had an uneasy feeling about the whole thing.

It was noon on a pleasant June day, with a high, blue, winter sky and a few puffy clouds. After the early winter rains, the terraces were sprouting with new growth and the paddocks had lost their all-over dry look. Today a stock agent was acting for Connor at the Strathalbyn cattle market and, as a result, the first herd of Herefords would be delivered tomorrow, probably at the crack of dawn.

Two stockmen would care for them and act as support for the gardener when needed. Connor, it appeared, had decided that he was not going to buy into the stud cattle business. Not yet anyway — he had neither the experience nor the expertise and he wouldn't have the time to supervise a proper breeding program. He was happy to start with a commercial herd and see how it went. Bit by bit, Seymour Rise was being reinstated as a flourishing cattle property.

And here, beside the dining-room steps, the whitewashed walls of Elizabeth's courtyard were already patterned by the first tendrils of climbing clematis and jasmine planted in small flower beds. A kumquat tree and a dwarf lemon stood in half-barrels, one on each side of the steps and, in one corner, tinkling water dropped into a crystal-clear pool from a stone cornucopia. Elizabeth still had to decide on the garden furniture. 'It has to be just right,' she'd told Natalie, 'and I may have to take a trip to Adelaide.'

Overhead, shadecloth could be wound out on rollers to shield the courtyard on hot summer days. It would be a tiny oasis in the broad spread of the gardens.

And this afternoon, before it was dark, Connor would be treated to a viewing when he returned from Adelaide. And I, decided Natalie, will be elsewhere — by design.

It was not to be. She was still carefully tying a waving branch of clematis to one of the many small hooks cemented between the bricks, when she heard his car roar up the drive and brake in a flurry of gravel. Hastily, she completed the job and shot out of the wrought-iron gate to the back of the house.

She hadn't seen Connor since the day he'd ambushed her outside the unit and invited her to 'the function to end all functions' — his mother's amused comment — now only a week away. The time she had spent on the hospital grounds and tackling another landscaping job for a retired army colonel living in Gawler had meant their paths hadn't crossed.

Hamish had told her that all sorts of things were happening. There was extra furniture going into the house and stackable chairs being unloaded by the ballroom. 'There have been workmen in there all hours of the day, Nat, and painters, and now they're sanding and polishing the floor.' He'd not really taken a lot of notice because he had been working on the flower beds and palms around the new pool, he said. But he'd got the impression of a great deal of activity.

It looked as if it *would* be ready for Christmas-in-June and she was glad for Connor's sake. But now she scuttled to the pool area to see if Hamish was ready to knock off for today. Her car was in the local garage for servicing and she wanted a lift back. And she wanted it quickly.

He was nowhere to be seen — and neither, she noted with dismay, was his truck. She sat for a moment on the low wall by the rose garden, pondering her next move. She had work to do back at the office. She needed to get there. And if the essential nature of her early departure had something to do with the fact that she could now hear Connor's and Elizabeth's voices from the direction of the courtyard, then so be it, she thought.

She didn't have long to wait. The wrought-iron gate clanged in a manner that would have done the hinges no good at all, and heavy footsteps thumped along the path.

As he rounded the corner of the house, she was struck by the haggard look of his face. Three weeks seemed to have aged him ten years. She thought fleetingly of the staff crisis at his Melbourne office — but Elizabeth had told her that it had been sorted out to everyone's satisfaction. Whatever — he looked as though he was carrying the cares of the world on his shoulders.

And, overlying that, there was a suffused look of anger on his face. She braced herself.

He stood in front of her, his legs apart in the truculent stance she'd learnt to recognize. For a moment, he said nothing, breathing rather heavily.

'Whose idea was that?' He didn't need to explain and she didn't pretend to misunderstand.

'Mine,' she answered in a tiny voice.

'And why didn't you consult me?'

'It didn't seem necessary.' Her courage

was slowly increasing. What had she to lose in being assertive? As soon as the job at Seymour Rise was finished, they would not see each other again. And there was no way he could profess to be dissatisfied with the quality of the landscaping, so he couldn't damage her reputation.

'Oh, so it didn't seem necessary? And what if I'd had other plans for that area?'

'But you hadn't, had you?' she asked spiritedly, standing up, her chin tilting, daring him to disagree.

'As a matter of fact,' he started, 'I had. But that is not the point.'

'Then what is the point, Connor? It was what your mother wanted, she's paying for it all and you should be glad that it will be giving her so much pleasure. There aren't a lot of other things here for her — she needs something to expend her nurturing instincts on.' His eyes widened with anger and she wondered if, perhaps, she'd gone too far.

Why was he so angry? She saw another emotion in his eyes, mixed with the anger and, in a flash of awareness, realized it was guilt. His business had taken him away so often that Natalie had wondered what the point was of having an office here at all. He appeared to spend very little time in it.

There'd been times when Elizabeth had been alone for days on end. She missed her friends, she'd told Natalie. Having lived in Melbourne for forty years, she had a network of social contacts. The place here was safe; the security system saw to that. But there had been occasions when, as Natalie pulled away from the house to go home, she'd glimpsed the older woman alone in the large rooms. She was self-reliant, but Connor must now have realized that he had not been taking enough care of her needs.

Natalie's eyes flashed and she felt two spots of burning colour in her cheeks. He was treating her in a highhanded way, as if he were venting his anger about other things on her. She was being used as a scapegoat.

'I suppose it was Hamish that persuaded you to do this? Extra, lucrative work for him, and his bricklayer friend.' There was a slight sneer in his voice, a tone she'd never have believed could be there.

'He had nothing to do with it.' Her voice sounded shrill. 'He simply did as he was asked to do.'

Connor suddenly lunged forward and grabbed her wrist. His voice was low now, and a trifle surly. 'And does Hamish always do what he's asked to do? Is he always at your beck and call? When you both go back to your cozy house down the road, is it always a contented love-nest?'

Her jaw dropped and she stared at him, trying to understand what he was driving at.

His face was close to hers and now she glimpsed anguish rather than anger in it. 'Oh yes,' he said in that same low voice, growling out the words as if they hurt him to say them, but he was going to say them anyway, 'Mrs Partridge rabbits on at the drop of a hat — gave me quite a bit of information about you and Hamish.' He was still holding her wrist in a grip like a vice.

'You've quite shocked the lady, you know. Living with Hamish in the first place, without the benefit of a marriage certificate — she couldn't accept that. And then finding you'd spent the night here. Alone, with me — you didn't fool her! Really, Natalie Jensen, you should care more about your reputation!' And he flung her wrist away from him and walked away.

Her heart was hammering in her ribs and, at first, her voice refused to function. She stood gaping after him, trying to make sense of what he was saying. His back was hunched and he had stuck his fists into his pockets as he strode off.

She stood up and stumbled to the front of the house. The only car to be seen was his — the workmen must have finished for the day, like Hamish. She would have to walk home but that didn't matter. It was a fine day and it would give her time to assimilate the significance of his words.

The driveway had been bitumenized now, and the culvert looked sturdy and neat after the edges had been repaired and strengthened. As she turned into the main road leading to the units she was still grappling with the tumultuous thoughts engendered by Connor's harsh words. Her reputation? How many other people thought that she and Hamish were living together? Did she care?

Yes, she decided. As it happens, I do care. She didn't want any misconceptions circulating in the village. Perhaps she and Hamish had been a bit stupid. What had seemed a sensible arrangement might have been unwise.

There was no sign of Hamish's truck outside the units. Damn! How was she going to collect her car? It was to be ready at four o'clock. Perhaps he was at the office. She picked up the phone.

There was a strange note in Hamish's voice as he answered. Yes, he was here — and that's fairly obvious, thought Natalie, irritated. Yes, he could come back and pick her up. And he wanted to introduce her to someone.

Natalie shrugged and put down the phone. And ten minutes later the truck pulled up and Hamish got out, practically ran around to the passenger side and opened the door. Natalie saw him carefully help down the dark-haired woman whom she recognized from the night of the play.

His face was red with excitement and his eyes were shining as he shepherded the woman inside Natalie's living-room.

'Nat, I want you to meet Marie.' Natalie hid her feeling of surprise as she shook hands with the pretty woman who, oddly, looked a bit hostile. Now what? I've had enough hostility for one day, she thought. I want someone to give me some TLC.

'Nat — ' Hamish could hardly speak for excitement. He started again. 'Nat, I want you to be the first to know. Marie and I are going to be married!'

★ ★ ★

'I realized something was different when I met her by accident two weeks ago, Nat,' said Hamish later that evening. 'She invited me to a party the pistol club was putting on. I was staggered,' he shook his shaggy head in wonderment, 'but I was even more staggered when she made it clear she wanted to continue the — ah — relationship.'

'I'm happy for you, Hamish. And I'll look around for somewhere else to live — it might be politic!' She could guess what the hostility had been about. Marie and Mrs Partridge and Connor had all jumped to the same conclusion.

Hamish was a little embarrassed. 'As

a matter of fact, Nat, it was our being together here that made Marie realize that she — ' The big fellow blushed and Natalie hid a smile. 'Well, it sort of woke her up to realize what she felt — ' He was stumbling over his words but he was making sense.

And, finally, her thoughts were making sense too. Could it be that Connor . . . ? She turned away from Hamish, clenching her fists to stop their trembling. His words came back to her, pounding into her brain like bells ringing out a message: 'When you both go back to your cozy house down the road, is it always a contented love-nest?'

10

'I'm glad you're coming to the party, Natalie,' said Elizabeth, giving her a little hug. 'For a lovely girl like you, there should be more parties. It sounds as if it will be quite something. A group to play for the dancing, caterers from Gawler organizing a smorgasbord and — a personal indulgence — a Christmas tree! I found a nursery selling Norwegian spruces — the real thing. It's only two metres high but I'm having great fun decorating it — had to scour Adelaide to find the baubles. Out of season, they told me.'

Natalie smiled at the older woman's enthusiasm. She'd had a wonderful trip to the big city, she'd told Natalie. Found exactly the right garden furniture she wanted for the courtyard, 'And, would you believe, I was having coffee one day in David Jones and

I bumped into an old friend of mine from Melbourne. Haven't seen him for years but we recognized each other right away. Maybe Australia isn't such a big place, after all!' She'd invited him to the wing-ding, she said, and he'd be staying at the pub in Ashley for the weekend.

A plan had been forming in Natalie's mind. A plan that involved a certain dark green velvet ball gown, just waiting to be flaunted. The party was the day after tomorrow and Natalie had casually told Connor, on the brief occasion that she'd seen him, that she was able to come after all. He'd simply inclined his head in an equally casual nod.

She'd have to move out of her half-house soon, but she'd had a long talk with Marie and had tactfully cleared up a few misconceptions. She quite liked Marie, she decided — she was just right for Hamish. Small and delicate, to bring out his protective feelings, but with a steely determination that would enable her to organize him when organizing was needed. Natalie smiled to herself as she scanned the short 'Flats to Let' column in the local paper. He'd got what he wanted and she could only hope he'd always want what he'd got.

* * *

'Now, Natalie, tie a scarf around your head and don't you dare get the bathroom steamy when you shower!' Annette, of Annette's Hair Concept — a somewhat fancy name for Ashley clients but since she was the only hairdresser, it didn't seem to matter — lightly twisted the last tendril into place. She'd left most of Natalie's hair smooth in a corn-coloured sweep to the back of her head, with two combs to hold up the sides. From just above each ear a wispy ringlet brushed her cheeks and from the combs the shining hair tumbled in a riot of ringlets onto her shoulders.

'It's a bit old-fashioned, Natalie. Are

you sure it's the way you wanted?'

'I'm just an old-fashioned country girl, Annette, and it's exactly the way I wanted.' It wouldn't last, of course. After one night's sleep it would be back to its normal swinging straightness. But one night was all she needed.

At seven-thirty, she stared at herself in the wardrobe mirror. 'Just give me a candle again,' she murmured, 'and I'll be the most romantic sight around.' She'd carefully applied the minimum of make-up but she'd not skimped the eye shadow. If there were to be brilliant lights in the ballroom, her delicate colouring would be swamped. In the bright light of her bedroom, she decided she'd got it right, and a soft rose lipstick complemented the glow of excitement in her cheeks.

She walked carefully out of the house, not wanting to muddy the hem. Hamish had left earlier to meet Marie. It was an unseasonably warm night, and that was good. She didn't have to ruin the image by throwing on a mud-spattered parka.

She'd keep the windows of the Suzuki closed for warmth.

The gravel parking area was almost full when she pulled up and there were lights everywhere, in the house and shining from the high windows of the ballroom. The covered path joining the house to the ballroom had fairy lights looped between the branches of the wisteria. She could hear the rhythmic beat of the musicians' instruments and there were people coming and going from cars to the huge room.

Suddenly she felt nervous. She knew only Connor and his mother, and they would have to be keeping an eye on the guests. Would she be wandering around on her own?

What if she had misread his feelings that day when he'd confronted her over the courtyard? What if he hadn't felt just like Marie had, when she thought Natalie and Hamish were an item? What if he gave her one quick, disinterested look and turned to someone else? There were some gorgeous creatures tripping along the covered path and they were wearing the most breathtaking gowns. Had she been foolish in thinking that there was still something between Connor and herself that had been merely held in check by misunderstandings?

'There is only one way to find out,' she decided and stepped resolutely out of the Suzuki, holding her skirt bunched in one hand.

She entered by the high front door. And immediately saw Elizabeth talking animatedly to a white-haired elderly gentleman who seemed to be hanging on to every word she uttered. The old friend from Melbourne, Natalie surmised. The woman turned around and gave a little welcoming cry.

'Natalie! You look absolutely marvellous! Doesn't she, Andrew?' And Andrew took his eyes away from Elizabeth for enough time to give Natalie an appreciative look before he turned back to Connor's mother. Smitten, thought Natalie, totally smitten.

And it wasn't surprising. Elizabeth was dressed in a simple, black, soft crepe dress, highlighted with a sparkling brooch on the shoulder and earrings to match. Her white hair curled softly around her laughing face and she looked ten years younger than when Natalie had first seen her.

'Now, where's Connor? He was here a moment ago. Natalie, be a dear and see if he's in the drawing-room. He went in there to check on the fire, but there are so many people arriving now that I can't cope with them on my own.'

Natalie made her way slowly towards the room she knew so well. Well, I'm only doing what his mother asked me to do, aren't I? As long as he doesn't think I am deliberately seeking him out. I must be subtle in my machinations.

He was alone, standing with his back to the door and staring into the fire, his hands in the pockets of his evening suit. She watched him for a moment. The broad shoulders were hunched under the black jacket, the long legs apart. She was silent, absorbed in the sight of the man who had taken her uncomplicated life in his strong hands and made it as complicated as all-get-out.

He must have sensed her presence because he turned slowly. She took a deep breath at the sight of him, the black tails cut away over the long, trousered legs and the ruffles of his snowy-white dress shirt contrasting breathtakingly with his tanned face and dark eyes. If anything, his beard looked more virile than ever. She wanted to bury her fingers in its bristly depths.

As he caught sight of her in the doorway, he gasped. His eyes gazed at the picture she made as if he couldn't believe it. For a moment there was silence in the room, broken only by the sudden fall of a log in the fireplace and the spatter of sparks flying up the chimney. Then he took his hands out of his pockets and took a step towards her.

'You look — stunning!' Just three words, but the tone of his voice endowed them with such emotion that her stomach contracted. Now he dragged his gaze away from her face and it travelled slowly down to her creamy throat and over the soft swell of her breasts, their shape subtly outlined by the draped velvet. Not until he had surveyed the whole length of her body did his eyes return to hers. He took another step towards her and held out his hands.

As if she were sleep-walking, she moved towards him, the rich material swishing sensuously around her legs. Holding out her own hands, with the frilled sleeves of the gown adding an air of soft femininity, she met him breathlessly, clasping his warm hands in hers. They stood a short distance apart, each openly admiring the other one.

Then a sudden commotion behind her caught his attention and broke the spell. His eyes became neutral again.

Not cold, she was glad to see, but the fire had been tamped — to some extent. Such a blatant blaze of emotion would have caused comment from the crowd that spilled into the room.

'Connor, what a marvellous place! It's like something out of *House and Garden*,' came a strident voice behind her and a busty blonde swept past Natalie, to fling her arms around Connor. Natalie just had time to reflect that if the woman flung her arms about much more, she'd pop right out of the scarlet chiffon that seemed to start just above her waist and that floated around her in a frenetic swirl.

After that, a whole stream of people flowed past her, oohing and aahing over the room and filtering into the dining-room beyond. Connor gave her the slightest of resigned shrugs and turned to entertain his guests.

She would go back to his mother, she decided. He knew she was here and if he wanted to find her again, he could. But Elizabeth was nowhere to be seen and neither was her admirer.

Natalie felt more than ever alone. Food, she thought — the universal comforter — the smorgasbord in the dining-room. But she found she had little appetite even though the lobster, the cold sliced turkey, the smoked ham, the many bowls of hot vegetables in a *bain-marie* and the cold salads beckoned. Three hard-working chefs were ladling out the food and replacing the platters with more from the kitchen. There were mince-pies and, in a warming cabinet and waiting to be served, four huge Christmas puddings.

'You look lost! Can I tempt you?' A large, florid man held out a plate to her. 'I've mislaid my wife — temporarily, I hope — but I like to have someone to talk to.' She looked at him warily for a moment. We don't want any more misunderstandings, she thought, do we? But he seemed harmless and he was too interested in the food to be troublesome, she decided.

'I say, that's a smashing outfit you've

241

got on,' he said between mouthfuls of lobster salad. 'Reminds me of something — or someone,' he added with a slight frown.

'Florence Nightingale?' Natalie asked.

'Oh no, old Flo wouldn't have worn her hair like that. No, maybe it's a Rembrandt painting I have at home.' Just like that, she thought, a Rembrandt he has at home. He looked vague. 'Not too good on art,' he said, 'but I — '

' — know what I like,' she supplied with a small smile.

He roared with laughter. 'Just what I was going to say,' he chortled. 'It's a good investment,' he added, as if that closed the subject.

'What's a good investment, Alan?' came a low voice from just behind Natalie. So close that she nearly dropped her plate.

'Art, Connor, art. I was just telling — er — what did you say your name was?'

'Natalie, meet Alan Carslake. Alan, this is Natalie Jensen. We're going to get married just as soon as she sets the date.'

'Why, you old rogue! You didn't tell anyone . . .'

Not even me, Natalie thought dazedly, as Connor took the plate from her hand, handed it to Alan Carslake and, taking her arm in a tight grip, led her firmly away.

They moved resolutely through the drawing room — at least, *he* moved resolutely while she tried to keep up, her head whirling. Through the side door to the wisteria-covered walk and then under the tiny coloured-lights, his hand now firmly on the small of her back.

'Connor,' she squeaked, stumbling a little.

'Shut up, Natalie,' he responded in a kind but firm voice.

'Charming,' she muttered as he swept her into the ballroom, almost empty now that the supper break had encouraged people to move into the house. A lone pianist was still playing some nostalgic numbers — the group would be having a break, she guessed.

Without hesitating a moment, he pulled her to him so violently that he all but knocked the breath out of her. His arm held her close, so close that she could feel her breasts pushed hard against his jacket. His other hand, warm and allowing no argument, held hers against his shoulder.

For a full minute, they moved in time to the music, the near-empty dance floor ensuring that there were no collisions. Then he left her hand where it was and both his arms were holding her to him. The scent of his maleness made her close her eyes with — what? Desire? He smelt wholesome and musky and, with his arms holding her so close that she could feel the thud of his heart, her insides melted. 'Connor,' she whimpered, 'have a heart. This is too public a place for — '

His mouth came down on hers, silencing her complaints. For what seemed a lifetime, their lips clung, until her legs started to weaken from the forceful effect of his kiss. She had to hold on tighter to stop herself falling. His head moved back, and she looked into his brown eyes, now foggy with desire.

She hadn't noticed the pianist stopping, but suddenly she was aware of silence and looked dazedly around her.

'They've all gone,' he murmured unnecessarily, nuzzling her ear.

'Connor!' She summoned all her energy, giving him a slight push. It didn't do much good, but it enabled a modicum of sanity to return.

'Connor, what's happened? And what was that crazy statement you made to Alan Carslake back there?'

He put his cheek next to hers. It wasn't bristly after all, not when it was resting on hers — it was silky-soft and altogether acceptable. 'I've been a fool, Natalie, a high-handed, self-centred, blind-as-a-bat fool.'

'I totally agree, but that still doesn't

answer my questions.'

He released one of his hands and gave her a gentle slap on her behind. 'You're supposed to be reassuring me.'

She waited, not daring to hope. Then he gave a huge sigh and started to talk again. 'Mrs Partridge came in on that Monday, remember? Before I'd had a chance to see you again. She — um — chatted somewhat enthusiastically as we shared a cup of coffee. And when you seemed off-hand — and more — when we next met, I decided that Mrs Partridge must have been right — that you and Hamish were more than just colleagues.'

He shuddered, holding her close again. 'It came as a hell of a shock to realize that it hurt. It hurt so much I couldn't think straight. I felt guilty — do I mean guilty? Whatever, I wished I hadn't made things so — difficult — for you that weekend. Hell, I nearly seduced you!' He pulled his head back and looked at her with humorous eyes.

Natalie took a deep breath. 'You

wouldn't have had to put a lot of effort into it to succeed, actually.'

His eyes widened with delight but then he looked puzzled for a moment. 'But you — '

'I was confused and apprehensive, Connor. The last time I'd been seduced it — well — it didn't turn out too well,' she finished lamely.

He looked at her thoughtfully for a moment. 'So I guessed.' He put his cheek against hers again. 'So, for all these weeks we've been holding each other at arm's length. And I thought that my over-the-top ardour had ruined what had seemed to me to be a terrific developing relationship. A mutual admiration and appreciation society, you might say.'

'It seems to me we've both been listening to other people instead of each other — or our own hearts?' she asked, her hands around his back now, feeling the hard muscles under the material of the jacket. 'I thought Mrs Grant was your wife.'

'What?' He stood back and stared at her.

'Until she arrived, of course.' And she told him the whole story. He laughed until tears came into his eyes.

'Oh, my love, my love, that will teach you to eavesdrop,' he gasped finally, wiping his eyes.

'And that will teach you to gossip with the cleaning lady,' she retorted.

He took her hand and led her to the seats at the side of the dance floor. 'As a matter of fact, it was the cleaning lady who finally cleared things up. But not until this morning. She came in bursting with the news that Hamish MacIntyre was going to marry Marie Clements after all this time, and how Natalie Jensen was going to have to move out and that she'd been mistaken actually, because she'd just found out that there were two separate units, Mr Grant, and that there'd been no hanky-panky, it seems.' He paused for breath, a huge grin on his face.

'How was she sure there'd been no

hanky-panky, Connor?'

'Because Marie had cornered her in the supermarket and sorted a few things out. Her Hamish wasn't that sort of person, she'd told Mrs Partridge and she'd better not go round the town saying that he was.'

They laughed together, holding each other's hands as they shook with amusement. Then he became serious. 'And this evening, when you walked in that door, you did things to me that left me under no delusions about my feelings, Natalie.' He brought her hands up to his mouth and kissed the tips of her fingers. Her stomach reacted predictably.

'You looked — you *look* — absolutely glorious, exquisite — I can't tell you.' He tentatively lifted one of the ringlets with a finger. 'How did you get this effect?'

She laughed a little shakily. 'It wasn't easy.'

'It was all I could do not to rush you up the stairs and into the four-poster.'

'Four-poster? What four-poster?'

'The one in the main bedroom, that we'll be taking over as ours just as soon as we're married — and I'm not going to wait long for that.'

She smiled then, her face so full of love that he made a small, unintelligible sound and pulled her close. After he released her from a long kiss, she looked up at him again. 'But your mother — isn't that where she's sleeping?'

'Not for long, Natalie, not for long. Do you know, after all the effort we've put into making her comfortable here and — er — everything,' he gave her a crooked, slightly abashed smile, 'she's talking about going back to Melbourne.'

'The old friend?'

'The same. He proposed today and she hesitated about four seconds, I understand. Oh, and she said she hoped you would look after the courtyard for her, so that when she comes over here for holidays, she can potter in it.'

'You don't want to pull it down? You

said you'd had other plans, Connor.'

'I'll tell you about those later. But now, before the others come back, I want to show you something. Just sit there.' He stood up and strode towards the end of the dance floor, to where the group had been playing just in front of the stage. She'd been surprised that they'd not been *on* the stage, but there must have been some reason, she guessed. She watched him go, her throat constricted by emotion. He looked wonderful, and he'd always look wonderful. He was everything she wanted in a husband. And good-looking too, she thought, smiling inwardly.

He disappeared behind the red plush curtains and she frowned in puzzlement. What was he up to — he'd had an expression on his face like a small boy, trying to conceal his excitement.

As she watched, the curtains slowly parted. And, in the dim space behind them, she could see overhead apparatus that looked familiar. There were drooping cables and spotlights hanging from beams. There were the lower edges of backdrops she had seen many times and, at the side, staggered curtains that could be used to supplement the main one. She recognized all of it. It came from the theatre hall in the town, the hall that had been demolished. Gone for ever, she had thought. And here it was, recreating a new theatre and waiting for someone to use it.

As she shook her head in disbelief, the footlights burst into life, illuminating the space. And, on the back wall, a backdrop with a scene of a garden and terraces that stretched into distant paddocks to a majestic mountain that drew the eye. It was the view from Seymour Rise, reproduced in realistic colours and painted by the confident hand of an artist.

He was next to her again in the empty room, his arm around her waist, an anxious look on his face. 'What do you think?'

'What do I think? You ask me, what do I think? Oh Connor, what do you think I think?' She took his face in her hands and looked into his eyes. 'I think you are the most wonderful thing that ever happened to me. You rescued all that — for me?'

'One good turn . . . Remember my antiques?' He was laughing now, happy to see her joy at what he had done. 'Come and get a closer look.'

Together, hands linked, they ran up the steps at the side of the stage and she wandered through the collection of equipment still to be put into place. 'It's all here, Connor, every last bit of it.'

'I wanted it to be a surprise, but I thought you might see it being delivered or erected.'

'So that's why you looked odd when you talked about the er-ballroom!'

'I see I shall have to watch the expression on my face.'

'No, I'll watch the expression on your face, Connor Sebastian. You watch

253

me.' His eyes widened in amusement.

He reached for her, wrapping his arms around her and holding her close to him. 'I shall certainly be doing that — with great enjoyment! And I'll be working here much more, and when I go away, you'll be coming with me. Your business won't suffer if you're away for a while.'

'What about when The Limelighters are in the middle of a production?'

'I'll organize things to suit. And talking of productions, the plan I had for that space at the end of the house, that you plundered for the courtyard, remember?' She nodded. 'It was for a large rumpus room, with a rocking-horse and a doll's house and model railways and — But we'll have to find somewhere else.'

'Productions? What are you talking about, Connor?'

'*Our* productions, love-of-my-life! Pattering of tiny feet. Get it?'

With the footlights still holding them centre stage, Connor brought his lips down on hers. She slid her arms under his coat and felt the warm muscles of his back. She was almost delirious with happiness.

And in the shadows of the hall, his returning guests applauded madly.

THE END

**Other titles in the
Linford Romance Library**

SAVAGE PARADISE
Sheila Belshaw

For four years, Diana Hamilton had dreamed of returning to Luangwa Valley in Zambia. Now she was back — and, after a close encounter with a rhino — was receiving a lecture from a tall, khaki-clad man on the dangers of going into the bush alone!

PAST BETRAYALS
Giulia Gray

As soon as Jon realized that Julia had fallen in love with him, he broke off their relationship and returned to work in the Middle East. When Jon's best friend, Danny, proposed a marriage of friendship, Julia accepted. Then Jon returned and Julia discovered her love for him remained unchanged.

PRETTY MAIDS ALL IN A ROW
Rose Meadows

The six beautiful daughters of George III of England dreamt of handsome princes coming to claim them, but the King always found some excuse to reject proposals of marriage. This is the story of what befell the Princesses as they began to seek lovers at their father's court, leaving behind rumours of secret marriages and illegitimate children.

THE GOLDEN GIRL
Paula Lindsay

Sarah had everything — wealth, social background, great beauty and magnetic charm. Her heart was ruled by love and compassion for the less fortunate in life. Yet, when one man's happiness was at stake, she failed him — and herself.

A DREAM OF HER OWN
Barbara Best
A stranger gently kisses Sarah Danbury at her Betrothal Ball. Little does she realise that she is to meet this mysterious man again in very different circumstances.

HOSTAGE OF LOVE
Nara Lake
From the moment pretty Emma Tregear, the only child of a Van Diemen's Land magnate, met Philip Despard, she was desperately in love. Unfortunately, handsome Philip was a convict on parole.

THE ROAD TO BENDOUR
Joyce Eaglestone
Mary Mackenzie had lived a sheltered life on the family farm in Scotland. When she took a job in the city she was soon in a romantic maze from which only she could find the way out.

NEW BEGINNINGS
Ann Jennings

On the plane to his new job in a hospital in Turkey, Felix asked Harriet to put their engagement on hold, as Philippe Krir, the Director of Bodrum hospital, refused to hire 'attached' people. But, without an engagement ring, what possible excuse did Harriet have for holding Philippe at bay?

THE CAPTAIN'S LADY
Rachelle Edwards

1820: When Lianne Vernon becomes governess at Elswick Manor, she finds her young pupil is given to strange imaginings and that her employer, Captain Gideon Lang, is the most enigmatic man she has ever encountered. Soon Lianne begins to fear for her pupil's safety.

THE VAUGHAN PRIDE
Margaret Miles
As the new owner of Southwood Manor, Laura Vaughan discovers that she's even more poverty stricken than before. She also finds that her neighbour, the handsome Marius Kerr, is a little too close for comfort.

HONEY-POT
Mira Stables
Lovely, well-born, well-dowered, Russet Ingram drew all men to her. Yet here she was, a prisoner of the one man immune to her graces — accused of frivolously tampering with his young ward's romance!

DREAM OF LOVE
Helen McCabe
When there is a break-in at the art gallery she runs, Jade can't believe that Corin Bossinney is a trickster, or that she'd fallen for the oldest trick in the book . . .

FOR LOVE OF OLIVER
Diney Delancey

When Oliver Scott buys her family home, Carly retains the stable block from which she runs her riding school. But she soon discovers Oliver is not an easy neighbour to have. Then Carly is presented with a new challenge, one she must face for love of Oliver.

THE SECRET OF MONKS' HOUSE
Rachelle Edwards

Soon after her arrival at Monks' House, Lilith had been told that it was haunted by a monk, and she had laughed. Of greater interest was their neighbour, the mysterious Fabian Delamaye. Was he truly as debauched as rumour told, and what was the truth about his wife's death?

THE SPANISH HOUSE
Nancy John

Lynn couldn't help falling in love with the arrogant Brett Sackville. But Brett refused to believe that she felt nothing for his half-brother, Rafael. Lynn knew that the cruel game Brett made her play to protect Rafael's heart could end only by breaking hers.

PROUD SURGEON
Lynne Collins

Calder Savage, the new Senior Surgical Officer at St. Antony's Hospital, had really lived up to his name, venting a savage irony on anyone who fell foul of him. But when he gave Staff Nurse Honor Portland a lift home, she was surprised to find what an interesting man he was.

A PARTNER FOR PENNY
Pamela Forest

Penny had grown up with Christopher Lloyd and saw in him the older brother she'd never had. She was dismayed when he was arrogantly confident that she should not trust her new business colleague, Gerald Hart. She opposed Chris by setting out to win Gerald as a partner both in love and business.

SURGEON ASHORE
Ann Jennings

Luke Roderick, the new Consultant Surgeon for Accident and Emergency, couldn't understand why Staff Nurse Naomi Selbourne refused to apply for the vacant post of Sister. Naomi wasn't about to tell him that she moonlighted as a waitress in order to support her small nephew, Toby.

A MOONLIGHT MEETING
Peggy Gaddis

Megan seemed to have fallen under handsome Tom Fallon's spell, and she was no longer sure if she would be happy as Larry's wife. It was only in the aftermath of a terrible tragedy that she realized the true meaning of love.

THE STARLIT GARDEN
Patricia Hemstock

When interior designer Tansy Donaghue accepted a commission to restore Beechwood Manor in Devon, she was relieved to leave London and its memories of her broken romance with architect Robert Jarvis. But her dream of a peaceful break was shattered not only by Robert's unexpected visit, but also by the manipulative charms of the manor's owner, James Buchanan.

THE BECKONING DAWN
Georgina Ferrand

For twenty-five years Caroline has lived the life of a recluse, believing she is ugly because of a facial scar. After a successful operation, the handsome Anton Tessler comes into her life. However, Caroline soon learns that the kind of love she yearns for may never be hers.

THE WAY OF THE HEART
Rebecca Marsh

It was the scandal of the season when world-famous actress Andrea Lawrence stalked out of a Broadway hit to go home again. But she hadn't jeopardized her career for nothing. The beautiful star was onstage for the play of her life — a drama of double-dealing romance starring her sister's fiancé.

VIENNA MASQUERADE
Lorna McKenzie

In Austria, Kristal Hastings meets Rodolfo von Steinberg, the young cousin of Baron Gustav von Steinberg, who had been her grandmother's lover many years ago. An instant attraction flares between them — but how can Kristal give her love to Rudi when he is already promised to another . . . ?

HIDDEN LOVE
Margaret McDonagh

Until his marriage, Matt had seemed like an older brother to Teresa. Now, five years later, Matt's wife has tragically died and Teresa feels she must go and comfort him. But how much longer can she hold on to the secret that has been hers for all these years?